The Healer of Harrow Point

The Healer of Harrow Point

For Tyler –
I hope you like the story —

Peter Walpole

Cover design by Mayapriya Long
Cover art by David Brown

For information write:

Hampton Roads Publishing Company, Inc.
1125 Stoney Ridge Road
Charlottesville, VA 22902

Or call: 804-296-2772
FAX: 804-296-5096
e-mail: hrpc@hrpub.com
Web site: www.hrpub.com

If you are unable to order this book from your local
bookseller, you may order directly from the publisher.
Quantity discounts for organizations are available.
Call 1-800-766-8009, toll-free.

Library of Congress Catalog Card Number: 99-95402

ISBN 1-57174-167-4

10 9 8 7 6 5 4 3 2 1

Printed on acid-free paper in Canada

For Dr. Jane Raymond Walpole
the best of traveling companions

Chapter 1

I remember there was a fine blue sky and a light brisk breeze on that first, beautiful late fall day when I met Emma. I was lying belly down in a nest of leaves in a little dry creek ditch, maybe twenty feet away from an almond-eyed, dusty-brown buck. His antlers were short but legal, meaning they were long enough, that the buck was old enough to be legally hunted once deer season began. He was safe now, I thought. Safe for a few more weeks. He was nosing about in a scraggly berry bush, tearing off small bits, munching the berries; little pieces fell to the earth around him as he chewed rapidly, his head bobbing from side to side. Then he nosed in and tore off another bit of the bush.

For a moment I felt supremely, wonderfully alive. I loved the cool crisp air and the dank smell of earth and leaves; and I loved the buck, rather like a collector would love a rare, long-sought-for piece for his collection. I had found him and he was mine. But a question, one that had been growing in me for months, picked at me, pulling back from the joy of that moment. If I had a gun, could I shoot him? Could I possibly squeeze a trigger and bring him down? It scarcely seemed possible.

When I reached the age of twelve, in six long weeks, my father was to give me my first shotgun and take me hunting for the first time. My birthday and the first day of hunting season would coincide, so we would make an outing of it, my father and I and a couple of his friends. There were times, when I was with my father or with my friends at school, that I was certain I wanted to go hunting when my birthday came. There were other times, chiefly when I was alone in the woods, that I was just as certain that I could never want to hunt.

I loved tramping through the woods. In long, rambling walks through the ancient forest land that surrounded my home town, my father taught me the rules of hunting, the ins and outs of tracking deer, the habits of wildlife. My father used these walks to scout the best places to hunt. He told me, clearly and unequivocally, that I was not to walk in the woods alone during hunting season. There was too much danger of being shot accidentally by a hunter. It was one of his few hard and fast rules. All the rest of the year I was free to wander as I pleased. So, there were many, many days when I would head off into the woods after school, to walk the places that I knew, to explore.

On Saturdays, my mother would often pack me a couple of sandwiches, and I would spend the whole day in the woods, the great source and playground of my imagination. Sometimes I was an Indian, moving quietly through the woods tracking a panther that was threatening my tribe; and sometimes I was Daniel Boone, pioneer woodsman and Indian fighter. But as I got a little older, it seemed that I imagined less and watched and listened more. The woods were more wonderful in themselves than anything I could imagine about them. It is difficult to explain, but I felt somehow that if I was quiet enough in my heart and in my head then I could become in some sense transparent, invisible even. I could slip through the trees like a spirit, watching and listening to all the wonders going on around me. There was a quiet there that went beyond the hushed and intricate sounds of the forest, a quiet that went deeper and deeper until it disappeared past hearing, past everything.

I had been so still watching that buck, my breath, my heart working on in perfect silence, and then I thought about shooting him, about whether I could possibly want to shoot him, and the silence was gone.

The buck looked up just as I did. On the ridge far above us a man in a red plaid shirt snapped a twig underfoot in the moment he leveled his rifle on target. He was a poacher, hunting out of season. I screamed as the sharp pop of the rifle cut through the air. The deer lurched back toward me, staggered once trying to keep its slim legs beneath it, and fell to the earth, not four feet from where I lay, dazzled by fear. His eyes were open, staring at nothing. His side was torn and bloody. His chest heaved twice with two great rasping snorts, a rippling shudder cascaded along his side, and then he was absolutely still.

I saw the man begin the difficult descent down the ridge. I wanted to get up and run away, and I wanted, I don't know . . . I wanted to scream at the man, to bash him with something, a tree branch, anything. More than all of that, more than all the world, I wanted the buck to rise and run off, unharmed, alive. I would follow him and find him and he would be mine again.

In the moment of that supreme wish I heard a crashing noise behind me, the sound of someone running, someone heavy, coming toward me. In a blur a figure rushed past me. It was a woman, heavy but not fat, older than my mother, I sensed, but not much older, in old, dirty pants and a weathered, heavy flannel shirt. She knelt by the deer, seeming almost to fold her large bulk around the fallen animal. She held its head up in her left hand, and stroked its coat with her right. Her eyes closed. She placed her head softly against the side of the deer. I dared not move. With a start the woman's eyes opened. She turned and looked directly into my eyes. Her eyes were a piercing blue. She seemed intensely alive to me—I don't know how else to describe her—in that instant when our eyes met. Then she closed her eyes and again inclined her head closer to the deer.

"Come now," she said quietly. "Come on. Up with you."

I didn't know what to do. I thought at first she was talking to me, but I was too afraid to move. I just watched as she roughly stroked and rubbed the buck's coarse fur. Her fingers went over the bloody wound in the deer's neck and she winced with pain.

"All right," she said, her voice quiet, tight. "All right."

In an instant something happened. The woman blew out a sharp breath and pushed herself from the deer, rocking back on her heels. The small buck twitched, rolled back and forward once, struggled to his feet, and then bolted off through the underbrush, leaping now to the left, now to the right with astonishing speed, far down the ravine, and was gone from sight. Struck dumb with wonder, I looked back toward the woman and saw behind her the hunter approaching, fifty yards away or so.

"Hey!" the hunter called. "That's my deer. You leave that alone!"

A dark frown passed quickly across the woman's face. She turned and looked at me.

"Run," she said. "Now."

"Are, are . . . are you," I couldn't quite get a question together in my mind, but I did manage to get to my feet. I took a step toward home and looked back at the woman. I was held in place by what had just happened.

"It's not safe here," she said quickly, a firm tone in her voice. "Run!"

But I just stood there, and the hunter was getting nearer.

"Oh for heaven's sake," she said, slowly and loudly. She stepped over toward me, pulled me out from behind the bit of brush where I had been hiding, and then scooped me up under one arm. She hefted me once for balance, and crashed off into the woods carrying me like an oversized football.

It is kind of comical to think of now, but then I was terrified, whizzing through the brush headfirst, my legs dangling behind. I could hear the great panting and grunting of the woman as she carried me. I was too big for her to carry me very far, and soon we were running side by side, crashing through the brambles and brush, her hand firmly grasping my arm.

Finally, the woman slowed to a trot, then a lurching, uneven walk, and finally pulled up at the base of a low hill covered with thick, sharp brambles. Her chest was heaving. She rubbed her left forearm across her face, wiping away the sweat. Then, looking as if she were surprised to find me there, tight in her grasp, she gently pushed me away from her.

"Oh pheewuu, oh my," she said, grinning, leaning down with her hands on her knees. "Oh, I'm getting—" she hiccupped "—old."

She shook her head, sat down with a crash, and, with some difficulty, propped herself against a small outcropping of rock, where she sat to recover her breath. As her breathing gradually eased, she began to eye me with apparent curiosity. I stared at her, too scared to talk or walk or do anything. A few more moments passed. It was odd, how quiet everything had suddenly become. I had no idea how far we had run; it seemed to be miles, but of course it couldn't have been. She was still looking at me. It made me feel strangely shy. I walked a very few steps away from her and then spun drunkenly on my feet. I stood still, and squinted at her.

"Well?" she asked, her breathing almost returned to normal.

I said nothing.

"Hmmph." She seemed utterly dissatisfied with me. My face was cut and scratched in a dozen different places after our run through the woods. I'm sure I was filthy from lying on the soft, moist earth. I imagine I was crying. The woman's look might have softened, although still she was eyeing me critically.

"Here," she said, "give me a hand."

Somehow I could follow a direct instruction. I took her large knobby hands in mine and tried to help her to get up from where she sat. She nearly pulled me over on top of her, but, in stages, I helped her up to her feet.

"Stand still," she said, and drew me a bit closer to her, taking my face in her hands. "Think of, oh, I don't know . . . strawberries."

"Strawberries?" I thought. Then I had the oddest feeling of my skin retracting, tightening, tingling. I knew that all my cuts were gone. She seemed to smooth them away like someone brushing wrinkles from a crisp, clean sheet.

"What is your name, young man?"

I was touching my face, bewildered that the scratches were gone.

"Thomas, ma'am," I said automatically, "Thomas Singer."

"Don't ma'am me. My name is Emma."

"Yes'm—Emma."

"Well?" she asked.

I looked all about, a little frantic. I didn't know what she wanted from me.

"Out with it," she snapped. She was quite brusque. I felt afraid of her.

"That deer," I said, finally. "That deer was dead."

"Surely not," she said. "You saw it run off."

"No," I said. "No, you did something."

"You think so?" she asked. "I don't see how."

"You did," I said, frowning.

So we stood there, at this first impasse, staring at each other; and I found in that moment that I was no longer afraid.

"I'm not sure what to do with you," Emma said, just barely out loud.

I felt a surge of confidence. I don't know why.

"I want to know what you did to that deer," I said emphatically.

She smiled. She might almost have laughed. "I'm sure you do, young man," she said, with a certain sharpness in her voice.

She started walking away from the base of the low, bramble-covered hill where we had been talking. I followed after her. I fixed my eyes on her boots, large, heavy hiking boots encrusted with red mud, and kept pace as best I could. I was tired and confused, but I was determined to stay with her. We walked quite a while, heading back toward where the deer had been shot.

"Do you walk out here often?" Emma asked me, in more of a conversational tone of voice.

"Yes ma'am . . . yes Emma," I said, correcting myself.

"So you know how to get home from here?" she asked.

"Oh, sure," I said, nodding.

"Then go," she said flatly. She was walking straight ahead, not looking at me.

I stopped in my tracks. That was not what I had expected her to say, not what I wanted her to say. She kept on walking. She was heading north; I would need to veer back the way we had come.

"Do you think he's still there?" I hollered after her.

She stopped, some thirty feet ahead of me now, and called back over her shoulder. "Who?"

"That poacher."

She turned and looked at me. It was a ploy on my part. She knew it, I'm sure. The woods were very quiet. The sun was starting to go down, low against the trees, and the air seemed to chill second by second.

She walked back toward me, slowly, heavily, her footfalls loud in the quiet air.

She stood in front of me, looming over me.

"You'll be fine," she said quietly. She reached out and touched my face again, lightly. Just as she pulled her hand away I felt a kind of shock, like she had shuffled across a rug and touched me. She was looking at me so intently, so gravely, as if inspecting me for construction flaws.

"If you walk out here some afternoon, we might see each other," she said simply.

I nodded.

"Now go home, Thomas Singer."

There was an emphasis in her voice that would brook no dispute. I nodded again and turned to go. I walked a while, up around the long, low base of the hill, pulling myself along. I looked back and she was still there, watching me, seventy yards away now, perhaps farther. I waved to her, sort of a broad, cheery wave. I felt odd. I didn't want to go home yet. I felt warm, deeply, uncomfortably warm on such a cool late afternoon. My hands especially felt warm. I kicked at the ground with the toe of my shoe. At that moment nothing felt quite right.

She was standing very still, watching me. I turned and took another few steps toward home and then gave her one last look back over my shoulder. She had her right hand raised, somewhere between a wave and a benediction. I waved again, quickly, briefly, and began the long walk home more in earnest, feeling slightly, slightly better, but still altogether too warm.

Chapter 2

I walked along slowly through the deepening twilight. Can one feel deeply perplexed and happy at the same time? I was trying to remember everything that had happened, and was trying, without the least success, to make sense of what I remembered. Emma had entered my life with such force; it didn't seem possible to me that so much had happened in the space of only a few minutes. I felt like I needed more time, that everything should have taken more time. I was sure I had a hundred questions to ask Emma, though perhaps, at that moment, I couldn't have formulated even one. I wanted to be with Emma. I didn't want to go home.

I gave a wide berth to the base of the ridge where the deer had been shot, where I last saw the poacher. I don't suppose I really thought he would still be around. There was a cloudiness in my mind, a mist that I thought Emma might be able to clear away; but I didn't want to go back to where that afternoon's events had begun. Still, I didn't want to go home either. It was starting to get dark, and very cold, but I continued to feel oddly warm. I walked slowly, looking around, listening. I didn't know what I was looking or listening for. Finally, I started to feel the cold, feel it sharply, and my pace quickened.

Thinking of home troubled me. My father always asked me about my day. I would be late for supper, I thought, and I was sure he would ask me about that. I didn't know what I would say.

I crested the hill that led to the open field at the edge of the little string of houses where we lived. We lived out in the country, but there were a few other houses around us. I could see the lights on in the MacCauleys' kitchen. No one was home at the Watsons' next door. Mr. and Mrs. Watson both worked at the grocery store in town, and I knew that they wouldn't be home for an hour or two yet. Seeing the MacCauleys' house lit up, and the Watsons' dark, was somehow a comfort to me; it was normal.

I was cutting across the wide field that climbed up to the back of our house. The lights were on inside. Mom was home. Just as I stepped over the narrow ditch that marked the back of our yard, I saw Dad's patrol car pull into our drive. I wasn't as late as I thought. I started climbing the slight incline, past my mother's garden, as my father got out of his car. I saw him wave to me. He was standing at the bottom of the drive, a good ways above me still. It was dark, but even so I could see the easy way he was standing, and it made me feel good, made me feel safe. How, in the dark, without him calling to me, could I tell that he was glad to see me, that I wasn't late, that everything was fine?

My father was an immensely practical man. He could fix cars, make end tables, cook breakfast. I suppose, really, when I was eleven it hadn't yet occurred to me that there might be things he didn't know, or things he couldn't do. He was strong and practical and friendly. It seemed that he could talk anybody into a peaceful, quiet mood, no matter how angry the person might have been to start with. He was a policeman, a sheriff's deputy in a large rural county. He was Deputy Singer, and I was Deputy Singer's son. Everyone, so far as I knew, liked him and respected him. I certainly did.

To me, it seemed that the things my father did were magic. How could he possibly know what was wrong with someone's car? I would stand beside my father, peering in at a dark, sooty, gray and black jumble of metal and tubing, mute with wonder. "Hmm," he would say. "What do you think, buddy?"

I never had a clue. I felt at once ashamed of my inability to grasp so many things about the world, and proud and somewhat in awe of my father's complete knowledge. He was patient in teaching me, about car engines, about all sorts of things; and I was determined to learn.

Among other things, my father was a hunter, a responsible and careful hunter. Of all forms of carelessness, he was least tolerant toward careless hunters:

hunters who fired their guns without being absolutely sure of their targets, hunters who did not know at all times where their hunting partners were. With my twelfth birthday approaching, we had been talking a lot about hunting and safety in the woods.

So, I was eleven going on twelve, and tried to be careful in all things. My father allowed me to roam the woods outside of hunting season, but still I knew he would be concerned to hear about the poacher. I didn't think I could tell him how near I was when the deer was shot. In a strange way, I felt as if I was implicated in the poacher's wrongdoing. And then, how could I possibly tell him about Emma?

When I reached the back door that led into the kitchen, I could see that my father was tired. He draped his arm around my shoulder.

"How you doin', buddy?" he asked.

I leaned in against his solid warmth. "I'm okay," I said.

He just nodded. I went to change and wash for dinner. When I came back into the big kitchen where we usually ate our meals, my father was telling my mother about one of the deputies: he was leaving to take a job up in Goochland County. My father was concerned because the Sheriff's department was already understaffed, and now they were losing another man. That would mean longer hours and more work for my father, and he didn't like it much.

My parents talked awhile, and I ate in silence, thinking about Emma, wondering where she was. I imagined her walking the woods, in the darkness, or maybe hunkering down somewhere to sleep. Where would she sleep? I thought of her like she was a bear, or some other creature of the wild. She certainly wasn't like any person I had ever met. I knew what I had seen Emma do, but I struggled to understand it. I set about imagining a world where Emma could walk the woods, healing injured animals with her touch. I wanted to be with her. I wanted to understand.

"How was your day at school?" my father asked. "I haven't said two words to you tonight, have I buddy?"

"It was fine!" I said, and it must have sounded like a protest or a claim of innocence because my father laughed.

"It's okay, sport," he said. "I didn't mean to startle you there."

"I was thinking," I said.

"What were you thinking about, Tommy?" my mother asked.

I shrugged. "I saw a deer today, in the woods," I said quietly. "I was, I don't know, I was wondering where it is now, what it's doing."

"Right now it is probably snuggled down at the base of some bush," my father said, "getting ready to go to sleep." My father sighed. "Lord, that sounds like a good idea."

"Why don't you go change out of your uniform?" my mother said to him. "Tommy and I will clean up."

"Do you mind, buddy?" he asked.

"No sir," I said.

As he got up from the table he reached over and gave me light sock on the arm.

"You're a good man," he said, a weary smile on his face. It was something he would say to me every now and then, and one thing about my father, I always knew that he meant it.

I helped my mother with the dishes and then went to my room to do a set of math exercises that were due in school the next day. I was already in bed when my father came into my room to say goodnight. He sat on the edge of my bed, and his weight, like it always did, tilted the mattress and rolled me toward him.

"You're too big for this bed, mister," I said, which is what I always said.

He smiled, and pulled the covers up around me a bit more, which I didn't particularly need. I pushed them back the way they were, and my father chuckled.

"Want to go down to Parker's with me on Friday?" he asked. "I need to pick up some things."

"Sure," I said. I loved going to Parker's.

"Great," he said. He leaned forward and gave me a light kiss on the forehead. Then he yanked the covers up over my head, and left the room with a quiet laugh as I howled in mock protest.

The next day after school I walked downtown instead of walking straight home. I had been thinking all day about Emma, about what I had seen, trying to think it through. I had some good friends at school, and one teacher, Mrs. Carlson, that I really liked, but I didn't feel like I could tell them about what had happened. It seemed special to me somehow, something that couldn't be talked about for fear of losing it or changing it.

Mrs. Carlson was my history teacher, a tiny, wiry woman who made everyone laugh. She was one of the smartest people I knew, but with a somewhat dubious logic I thought: what would a history teacher know about this sort of thing? What would anyone know?

And then I thought about Dr. Banks, the veterinarian. His office was downtown, just a few blocks from school. We had an old dog named Toby then, a little dachshund we had more or less adopted from my grandmother. Toby had never really been sick, but we took him to Dr. Banks for his shots and check-ups. Dr. Banks was somewhere in his sixties, I suppose, and that made him seem very old to me. I thought if anyone in town could help me right then, maybe Dr. Banks could.

When I reached his office I wasn't sure what to do. I had never before just dropped by there to visit. I didn't know Dr. Banks all that well. I stood on the sidewalk and thought for a few moments, and my resolve weakened. But when I walked past the side of his office, there was Dr. Banks, standing on the cement walkway that led back to the animal runs, hosing off a pair of large wading boots.

"Thomas Singer," he said with a crisp nod.

I was surprised he could place me so quickly.

"Hi, Dr. Banks," I said, and because it seemed the natural thing to do, I walked over to talk to him.

He was wearing a heavy pair of weather-beaten overalls. The boots he was washing had been covered with mud and muck.

"Being a country vet," Dr. Banks pronounced, "is messy work."

"Do you like being a vet?" I asked.

"Yes I do," he said. He reached over and shut the spigot off, and put down the hose. "You thinking of becoming a vet?"

I had never thought of becoming a vet.

"Maybe," I said, because it seemed the polite thing to say.

"It's hard work," Dr. Banks said. "It doesn't pay as well as some people seem to think, and the hours are long. But it has its rewards."

This seemed a set piece on his behalf. I nodded, and then spoke quickly, before I had a chance to think.

"Dr. Banks, do you think someone could heal an injured animal just by touching it?"

Dr. Banks was a good man; he considered my question seriously a moment.

"The laying on of hands," he said tentatively.

"Sir?"

"Part of the practice of medicine, the laying on of hands—touch, simple touch. You can calm an animal, a domestic animal that is used to being handled, by holding it, stroking it."

I frowned. "I mean, take a deer, an injured deer. Could someone . . ." and I simply stopped. On one level the question was consuming me, and yet I couldn't speak the words in a plain and direct way. On another level I already knew the answer; I had seen the answer myself.

Dr. Banks, who had a tendency to do or say slightly odd things now and then, seemed to hum or sing a snatch of a tune under his breath. I got only a muffled "that's for me" at the end.

"Sir?" I was confused. I didn't know if he was making fun of me.

"Have you ever been to one of those old tent revival meetings?" he asked me. "You know, I think they still have them now and then out at Meadow Falls. And they'll have some old time healings there, in the spirit of the Lord."

"Do you believe in that?" I asked, quite earnestly.

"These are matters you should discuss with your parents," Dr. Banks said, picking up his boots and turning to the side door of his office. "And I have patients to see."

"Okay, but Dr. Banks, just tell me this . . ." and again I was stumped. I just stood there, frustrated, feeling that I was close to something I needed to know. My fists were clenched at my sides.

Dr. Banks stood in front of me, impatient, forbidding. With a boot in each hand he swung them together lightly, so they just tapped, once, twice. Then he set the boots back down.

"I don't know how the body heals, Thomas," he said quietly. "I wish I did. There are things I can do for my patients, ways I can help them, but I've been around long enough to know that most of the animals that get better here pretty much heal themselves. And then some don't, you know; they don't heal themselves, they don't get better. They just . . ." he waved his hand vaguely in the air. He didn't say "die."

"And I've been to a couple of those tent meetings. Just to see, to watch. But I don't believe—"

I think I frowned. He shook his head, and continued, rapidly: "But that's not the point, what I believe. I think some of the people really are helped, really are helped to heal because they do believe. But I don't know how to make an animal believe, Thomas. It's a question I've rolled around in my head for some years. I try to be as gentle as I can with them, and confident, somehow, so they might sense that they are in good hands, but I don't know how to make them believe. So I don't know how anyone could help your deer. Not with only his bare hands."

I nodded, slowly, solemnly.

"Does that answer your question, young man?" Dr. Banks asked me, a little sharply; but I sensed a rough kindness in his voice.

"Thank you, sir," I said, and walked slowly away, and heard the side door of his office bang shut.

I walked down Main, looking at the sky. It wouldn't be light much longer. My pace quickened. I had about three or four miles to walk. It seemed I had more energy now, a lot more energy. I started to run, down where Main Street turned into Route 11 heading out of town. I plunged into the meadow land that bordered the town and led out toward the woods where I had met Emma what felt like years before. I was running as fast as I could, feeling as light and quick as a fast-moving stream.

I was laughing, my eyes tearing from the cold and from the run. I circled, at a slow, dizzy trot, the base of the bramble-covered hill, deep in the woods, where Emma and I had talked.

"Emma!" I shouted. Then I bent over, catching my breath. I didn't have to shout, I thought. She knows I'm here. I was certain she would show up any moment. I was grinning. I was grateful to Dr. Banks. I felt like now I had some very specific questions that I could ask Emma.

Of course, I was wrong. For all his generosity, Dr. Banks had not left me much wiser than I had been before. But I felt that I had broken through the husk of this question that had consumed me the last twenty-four hours. I felt elated. I looked around me. The light was starting to fade; the sky above me was a lovely deep cobalt blue, edging slightly deeper and darker, second by second. A light, cool breeze wrapped through the trees. An involuntary shiver passed through me.

"Emma," I said quietly, imploringly.

I hugged my arms around myself. I listened, strained to listen, to feel . . . something. My heart was pounding. I was too keyed up. There was nothing that I could feel. I waited another ten minutes or so, but Emma never appeared.

Chapter 3

After school the next day I went straight out to the base of that bramble-covered hill. I had had such a clear dream the night before, of Emma leaning over the wounded deer: if anything the dream seemed sharper, more real somehow, than the event itself. I could see her, the creases in her face, a wince of pain passing through her eyes, into her neck and shoulders, then fading. There was a look in her face of deep concentration, and of peace. In the dream, which stretched on and on as if in slow motion, I stepped over to her, leaned over behind her, reached out to place my hand on top of hers. And awoke.

I was determined to see her again. I waited in the woods until dark, frustrated, angry even when she did not show up, but determined to walk, walk, walk the base of that dull, scraggly little hill day after day until she appeared. I was there the next day, too, but by then my anger had faded, to be replaced, finally, by a long sorrow that left me sitting on a rock, the same rock she had sat upon days before, to catch her breath after lugging me through the woods. I was quiet, near tears. I wanted with all my heart to see her again.

The next day was Friday, and my father and I drove down to Parker's in my dad's old pickup truck. I was very happy. Somehow I couldn't be with my father and worry about seeing Emma at the same time. The truck was a great, noisy, smelly monster of a vehicle, as old as my father, or nearly so. He kept the cab clean, but still it smelled of oil and gas. The old, broad vinyl seat had a strange plastic musty smell of its own. We rocked and bounced down the road, unable to talk except by shouting, so we barely talked at all. It was okay, though. My father would look at me and grin now and then, that was all. In some ways that was all I needed in the world.

Parker's was a great old place. It was a country store of the old fashioned type, carrying just about everything a rural community could need. Parker's was in a cavernous old building that disappeared back from the road in various additions that had been tacked on over the years. The store was at a crossroads of sorts, just off the highway, and there was a little diner in the front, over on the side, where truckers would regularly stop and eat. Behind the diner was the general store proper, with groceries, lumber and hardware, toys and sporting goods. Some of the stock was so old it looked as if it hadn't been touched in years: Honus Wagner baseball bats, a faded red sled with rusted rails. You half expected to come upon a bottle with a shrunken head in it. Parker's was a great place for a kid just to wander around and look at stuff: a cheap beginner's banjo, a fat laughing china Buddha, enormous beer steins with different famous buildings molded into the glass—one the Eiffel Tower, another the Taj Mahal.

I walked and walked, picking stuff up, having a fine time, but eventually I made my way up front and found my dad in the hardware section. He was getting some clips to hold together part of a wire fence he was putting up at the base of our garden. My mother kept a vegetable garden, but the deer were getting into it worse than ever that year, so my father, in what little spare time he had, was going to put up a taller wire fence to replace the short cross board fence that even I could step over.

"Hey sport," he said to me. "See anything you just got to have?"

I shook my head. "No sir," I said. "'cept we have to get our pie."

He laughed. "No, we can't forget that. Here you go, then."

He handed me the bag of clips and he hoisted up some other things that he was going to buy, a heavy mallet and some pointed metal stakes for the fence, and we headed up toward the front of Parker's.

After my dad paid for everything and we took it all out to the truck, we went back inside to the diner. We settled into a booth and ordered burgers and cokes and two big slices of banana cream pie. The pie came on dinner plates, each slab a good three inches high. The banana cream pie was my favorite part of going to Parker's. I suppose it was the sort of pie only a child could love, but my father always made a sizable dent in his, too, before letting me finish his piece.

There were six or seven men in the diner that evening—truckers, mostly. I recognized a couple of them. My father might have known all of them, I imagine. We greeted each other and the talk flowed pretty easily. My father told them about the fence he was going to put up, and the trouble we were having with the deer.

"Those sons a' bitches will flat destroy a garden, won't they?" one fellow said.

"Well, they will," my father agreed.

"Better make that fence high," another man continued. "They'll hop right over it."

My father nodded.

"I know something that'll work better than a fence," the first man said. He held up his hands like he was holding a rifle. He crooked his finger and made the slightest little "click" sound with his tongue. Then he grinned at me.

"You going hunting this year, young fella?" the second man asked me.

"Yes, sir," I said quietly.

"First day of hunting season is his birthday," my father said.

"Is that so?"

"I gotta be on the road," the first man said, shaking his head. "Hate to miss the first day." He looked at me and sort of bugged out his eyes and cackled. "But I'll be right on their asses the day I get back."

My father smiled. He reached over a bit suddenly, almost awkwardly, and patted me on the upper arm. I was looking past him, out of the window, looking out at a wide, empty field across the road from Parker's, part of someone's farm that seemed to stretch back for miles. For a moment, for just a moment, I felt so sad and distant.

"How's your pie?" my father asked.

"The best," I said, pulling my attention back inside.

"I think I'm going to need some help here," he said, and nudged his plate toward me.

"Okay," I said, and glanced past his shoulder out the window again, not consciously really, and saw, for just a fraction of a second, the figure of a large woman striding along the edge of that distant field.

"I . . ." I think I was about to say, "I have to see something," but even that would have taken too long. I bolted from the booth and out the front door of Parker's, which brought me only twenty paces or so from the highway. A tractor trailer hurtled past in a roar of noise and swirling dust. I ran quickly to the left, trying to get the same angle I had had from the diner window. I looked out across the highway to the great, empty, rolling fields, one folded in behind another, for miles back to the base of a distant mountain range. Beautiful, vast, and empty.

The next morning was Saturday. I had made some excuse for my strange behavior the night before, and everything was fine between my father and me. He had to work that day, another twelve-hour shift, so I left the house early, right after breakfast, and headed straight out into the woods to the bottom of that same forsaken little hill, determined to stay there all day if I had to. I hadn't been there three minutes when I heard the sound of footfalls through the leaves, and Emma appeared from around the west edge of the hill.

"Good morning, Thomas," she said.

"Ma'am," I said with a nervous quake in my voice. She raised her eyebrows. "Emma," I corrected myself.

She nodded. She was carrying on her back a small canvas pack. She swung it off her shoulders.

"I have here a couple of peanut butter sandwiches, two apples, a few cookies, and some cider. My memory is that boys your age like peanut butter sandwiches."

She looked at me, questioning.

"Yes," I said. "Sure."

"Good," she said.

"Can I have a cookie now?" I asked.

"You may not," she said. "Would you like to go for a walk?"

This was not a question, I realized. I nodded and fell into step beside her.

"I came out here twice last week and you weren't here," I said, after we had walked a bit.

"Did you?"

"How did you know I would be here today?" I asked.

"I didn't know," Emma said, and for the first time I sensed a flicker of warmth from her. She almost looked shy, glancing over at me sideways.

"I hoped," she said.

That day began my friendship with Emma. Almost every afternoon, after school, I ran out into the woods to Tallon's Creek, followed it a mile or so to where it swamps, went north toward the mountains for another mile, then east down the rocks to the ravine where, at the base of that low, bramble-covered hill, we always agreed to meet.

In bits and pieces, over a period of days, she told me about herself, about her history. It was hard getting information out of her. She seemed much more interested in me, what my parents were like, what I learned in school, what I thought about things. I told her what I could, and in return I learned about her.

She said her full name was Emma Carter Crawford. She told me, very strictly, to call her Emma. She never did tell me why she didn't like to be called "ma'am." She had different quirks like that, I came to learn. Sometimes I would ask her a question, and wait for her answer, but none would ever come. She would just walk on as if I had never spoken. I couldn't tell if she didn't like the question, or was lost in thought, or simply hadn't heard me. Some of the time we were together we didn't talk at all. The two of us would walk along in the woods, mile after mile.

Other times she talked freely. She told me that for years she had worked in her family's hardware store,

Carter's Hardware in Harrow Point, a little town about ten miles from where I lived. Her father had built the store and run it for twenty-three years. When he died, she took over the store.

She married, she said, forty-seven years ago.

"He was a sweet man. People said he married me for my money—I owned the store when Papa died, and that was money in Harrow Point—but he didn't. He loved me. He couldn't change a light bulb, poor man, had no common sense at all. But he was a kind man. He loved me."

It seemed an important point to her, and I nodded solemnly.

After seven years of marriage she was widowed. Those years brought her three children: now all were grown and moved away.

I listened politely to her personal history. But what I really wanted to know about was what she had done with that deer. I pestered her with questions, which she more or less gracefully dodged, or else ignored altogether, the first few times we walked together. But one day, she admitted that yes, she had "helped" the deer. I wanted to know how; rather desperately, I wanted to know.

It was after we had been walking together for a couple of weeks or so that she finally told me about a visit she had had, at her store, many years before. One day, she said, a man had come to the shop a few minutes after closing. He was carrying an injured fawn. His name was Carlton Nash.

"I'd known him for years," she said. "At least I knew who he was. Everyone did. He was a local character. He said he was a hundred and two years old—no one knew how old he really was; eighty or so, we all thought. He didn't look all that old. He said he could talk to animals.

"There was a place in town called the Johnson Home for Adults, a kind of nursing home and, really, sanitarium. Mr. Nash had lived there—well, stayed there, now and then—for as long as anyone could remember. He said he had come down from Tikkun Ridge, up near the state line, years and years before. No one knew any different. He was a strange man, strange habits. He would wander off for weeks at a time, then just show up one day and settle back into his room.

"Sometime after my husband died, I guess I became a local character, too. I took in all sorts of strays: dogs, cats, and such. I had a mess of tame squirrels, a few rabbits. People began to bring me things: birds with broken wings and whatnot. Every so often Mr. Nash would limp along, his pockets full of milk bones and peanuts and little dry rolled pieces of oats and molasses. He had something for all the animals. He would sit on my porch or on the big stump in the yard, and in no time he would be surrounded by whatever animals were staying with me then. He would jabber away at them, and from where I watched, I believed the animals were jabbering right back. He never had much to say to me, though. Just the animals.

"And then one day he came into the shop, carrying the fawn.

" 'She's been hit by a car,' he said. He sat down on the window ledge, cradling the fawn in his arms. 'I'm getting too old for this. Think I might retire. So, you and me got to talk.'"

"Of course, I didn't understand what he meant."

"We spoke for hours," she said, "all night and through the morning. By noon, Mr. Nash was gone, and the fawn was healthy . . ."

She let the words hang in the air. She tried to let the story trail off, but there was no way I was letting her stop.

I plagued her with questions. The secret was half told, I believed, and I wanted to learn the rest. Over the days to come, gradually but clearly, forcefully even, she told me things, taught me things. Interspersed with stories of her life, questions about my days at school, and observations on the weather and such, she began teaching me about a part of life that was utterly new to me.

She told me that healing animals was a question of spirit, of spiritual strengths and hierarchies. I listened closely, and maybe understood a third, a fifth of what she said. Animals, she said, have great strength and beauty; spiritually, they are simple, however, and somewhat coarse. A human's spirit, she said gravely, is the greatest, finest, most powerful force in nature.

"A tragic truth," she said, and fixed me with a stare. Pay attention, her look said. This is important.

I learned early on that she had a way of looking at

you, now and then, that simply commanded attention. It wasn't a look she used often, but there was no resisting it. To that point in my life the only person I knew that commanded such respect was my father.

Again and again she emphasized the extraordinary power of the human spirit. She talked of it as being both a gift and a responsibility. But she said that I was not to think that animals did not have a power all their own. Integrity, she called it. She told me about a fox she found caught in a metal leg trap, a trap which had been meant for bear.

"His leg was mangled, just mangled. He had been there a while, and I thought the fight was about out of him. He looked terrible. I spoke to him gently, and touched his leg, and his eyes met mine and the jolt! It almost knocked me over backwards."

"Jolt from what?" I asked.

"From him. The simple, clean power of what he was. I hadn't met that in deer; they're such gentle creatures. There was power in that fox."

She shook her head. "It was all I could do to get the trap open and off his leg, and him fighting me all the way. Oh, he was strong, and not just physically, Thomas. His will was strong, his being. I was determined to do something for his leg and he was determined to have no part of it. I still don't know which of us was right. Sometimes I push too hard."

"Did you fix him?" I asked.

She shook her head again. "I helped him. That's all I can ever do, help. Here's what I got for my trouble."

She showed me her left hand. At the base of her palm there was a wide, whitish scar, and an indented place, like part of her flesh was missing.

"Did he bite you?" I asked.

She nodded. "Hard," she said.

"Couldn't you heal yourself?"

The question seemed to stop her. She shook her head.

"It's funny," she said at last. "I live this life, the things I do—but when it came to my hand, it's almost like I couldn't quite talk myself into it, couldn't quite believe it. I couldn't trust my own spirit, the way I impose my spirit on the animals."

We walked a while in silence.

"I was right to try to help that fox, Thomas," Emma said. "I don't know that I was right to insist."

"But you helped him," I said.

"It was a battle of wills. I won. I'm not saying I was wrong. Anyway, I'm hard-headed enough that I know I would do it again, if the situation were the same. But don't for a moment think that because your will is strong, these creatures don't have a perfect integrity of their own. An animal can be perfectly itself the way only the rarest of people can."

The point of her teaching was never the wonder, the magic of the healing, but the work of it, and the reasons behind it. She didn't want me to be in awe of her powers, or to be delighted in them as something magical. She was trying to get me to see, to really understand something of what she did.

Once she began to teach me, her silences grew deeper, and more frequent. Sometimes I could scarcely get her to talk to me at all. We would walk along quietly together. It seemed at times that she was looking for something, or listening for something. I learned just to let her be, not to bother her with questions. An hour might pass in silence, two hours, and then suddenly she would start to talk again.

To be honest, I had trouble following her. I would get used to the silence, enjoy it even, and then Emma would start teaching me, and I would struggle to understand her.

She was squatting at the top of a ridge one day, tossing little bits of bark onto the ground in front of her. She was squinting up at me, in this way she had, as if she was arguing with herself over something, something to do with me. I just stood there, shifting from one foot to the other, waiting.

"People have become so utterly, fundamentally convinced that spirit and matter are separate things," she said, "that certain essential human skills have been all but lost."

I frowned at her, squinted back at her. I wanted to understand.

"There is greater and lesser force," she said. "But there are no planes, no levels of existence, no spirit world, no lower realms. There is no spirit as opposed to matter, no matter separate from spirit. There is only life. I've thought about this for a long time, Thomas. It's not that I am so sure I'm right, but I want at least to tell you what I think. Okay?"

I shrugged. "Okay," I said.

"You see, people see one side of things, one facet of life—what they can immediately touch and see and feel. They think the spirit isn't real just because they don't think they can see it. But Thomas, understand, spirit is all you ever see."

She was looking at me hard. I don't know how much I understood. She shook her head.

"It's as if folks had decided that the right hand is stronger than the left, and so never used their left hand at all. And you know what would happen"—I did not—"the left hand, the human left hand, would just get weaker and weaker, until it seemed useless. And think, Thomas, what would become of people born naturally left-handed?"

I was eleven and I believed her, word for word, as well as I could follow her.

"Are you, you know, left-handed?" I asked.

"Hmm," was all she said.

"People use so little of their real spiritual potential," she told me. "They ease along on one percent, two percent in a crunch; for years they can drift along on nothing, nothing at all. Power can be given, infused. Mr. Nash was a great source of power. But you must be ready. Your spirit must be cultivated, strengthened, poked and prodded, stretched and battered about, educated, or an infusion of great power can burn you to a crisp."

Of course, everything she said was entirely new to me. I just listened in awe.

Another time I asked her more about how she healed animals. She said that the more seriously injured an animal was, the more time she needed to heal it, and the more draining the healing was to her strength. Time was important. The deer I saw shot was relatively easy for her to heal.

"But he was dead!" I said.

"Oh, that. Well, there's dead and there's dead. His body was strong, full of warmth and life. If he had been there a few hours it would have been a different story. I think I could have brought him back, but it would have taken a good long time.

"But then," she said, "you take a rabbit that's been run over by a car, crushed; well, then it doesn't matter. You have to have something to work with."

I blinked. I didn't want to think about crushed rabbits.

"But mostly it's just deer, somehow," she went on. "It's just deer that I find. Sometimes I think that certain things are simply given to you."

"How about people?" I asked. "I mean, if someone died—"

"No. I can't. Maybe some can. Mr. Nash said he had seen it, seen it from the woman who taught him. But he couldn't, and I can't. People are beyond me." She chuckled at that. "People are beyond me in a lot of ways."

"But my face, when I was scratched that day!"

"Oh, well, cuts, scratches, that's one thing. They don't really trouble you. But anything that truly frightened you, any serious injury where your spirit was shaken, or broken . . ." she just shook her head.

I looked down in despair. Once again I didn't understand.

"The world is more connected than you know," she said, in the slow, firm voice she used when she was trying to drill something into me. "You are what you see," she said.

"You are what you see," I said to myself, as if repeating the words would help me to understand them. Then I asked another question.

"So there was another, a woman before Mr. Nash?"

She nodded. "Yes. We go back for ages and ages, Thomas. We've been burned as witches, feared as sorcerers, revered as messengers from God . . . but usually completely ignored, unknown. And unknown is best, believe me."

I was fascinated and troubled by the things she told me. It seemed to me her power to heal was goodness itself, and yet still I was troubled. I believed everything she told me. For me there was no question of not believing her. I had seen her power with my own eyes, and thought that such power must be wedded to truth. I spent my days in a state of pleased confusion, happy to be friends with Emma, and trying to understand her and the things she said. I suppose in a way I am still working on some of the things she told me.

She was a large woman. Her face was weathered, red, shiny and smooth along her forehead and cheeks. Her eyes were bright and small, set in wrinkled pockets;

they glittered a deep, unsettling blue. Her hair was gray and blond, long and full, and frizzy at the ends, flying everywhere when it was loose, sticking out everywhere when she tied it back, wound tightly to her head. She was not inclined to smile, but occasionally she would grin at something, and chuckle, which was fine. When the weather was at all cold she limped when she walked. She was neither fat nor muscular, but solid, solid through and through. She said she was eighty-three. She said Mr. Nash really was a hundred and two.

"One of the compensations," she said, and waved her hand vaguely, "of all this, is aging comes a bit more slowly."

I nodded, as if I understood.

Our long, rambling walks covered the same forest land I had walked many times with my father. My legs were just sprouting that year, and I was always rushing on ahead of her, and being called back.

"Here," she would say sharply. "Now look at this."

She showed me the paths the deer took through the woods, where rabbits burrowed at the edge of woodland meadows, ponds where the deer came for water, and the tracks and the droppings of fox and bear. Her teaching reinforced my father's. Then it struck me: one reason I was troubled was because of how similar their knowledge was.

"Well, of course," she said, when I told her this.

"What do you mean?"

"Thomas, the deer I help go on to die, someday, somewhere. Some die of hunger, some of disease, some by hunters. I can't reach them all, only a very few. Some die of grand old age. But they all die. Now, here is something important to tell you: I could never kill an animal. I guess I would say I can't even understand how someone could kill an animal, but I won't go on to say that hunters are evil or heartless or savage."

"But . . ."

She shook her head, quite emphatically. "You want a simple world, but don't you see the turmoil inside you? You love your father, and yet now you think his hunting must be evil. But think deeply. Why are you troubled?"

"I . . . I don't know."

"Do you love him?"

"Yes," I said quickly, and I was sure I did, and yet I ached.

"Why do you love him?"

I didn't know how to answer her. "He's my father," I said simply.

"Exactly!" She actually smiled, and slapped me on the back. "Now think."

I could think of nothing else. It was less than two weeks until my birthday. I knew my present was to be a new, cut-down shotgun, and a fluorescent orange hunting coat. I knew that on the morning of my birthday I was supposed to take that new shotgun, load it . . .

I had a sick sense that I would simply go along, too afraid to resist. More than anything I was afraid that I wouldn't be able to decide, that I would be in anguish until the last minute, until . . . what?

I had this same nightmare, again and again. I would be walking in the woods with my father. I'd point at a deer, turning to tell my father, in a reasonable voice, "You see, I just can't," and in a blast of smoke and fire the deer would fall. I would realize with horror that I had been carrying a shotgun the whole time, that I had fired. With the logic of dreams I would be once again lying on my stomach in the ravine, watching the deer fall, only now it was I who had shot it. I lay there, sweating, my heart pounding, waiting for Emma to come, to set things right. She never did. The deer lay stiff and cold, its glassy eye staring blankly at its killer. At me.

I wanted to tell my father about the dreams, but I didn't. You have to understand about my father. He had such a commanding presence to me, and yet he was such a friendly, gentle man. He was the hardest person in the world to refuse, to argue with, to disappoint. I wanted to be with him and I wanted to be like him.

Well, of course, I didn't know what I wanted. I wanted to be like other kids, like older boys who went hunting. I could see the logic of it. Many deer die of starvation when they're not hunted. Hunting helps control the deer population. The occasional poachers notwithstanding, the hunting season was closely monitored by the game wardens. I knew all the arguments in favor of hunting. I had heard them all my life.

Also, there was the hunt itself: the men together, drinking coffee and laughing in the early morning, telling jokes, trying to keep warm. I would watch them out of my bedroom window each winter when hunting season came. They would be hugging themselves against the cold. I would see the frost of their breath as they talked and laughed. They would always start talking in whispers and end up hollering happily at each other, laughing, until they would remember that it was early, and their voices would fall, quiet laughter building more loudly again. Finally, they'd climb into two or three pickup trucks, and rattle away. Late in the day they would return, with more laughter and talk, full of stories of the day.

To be a man was to be with them.

Often, of course, at the end of the day, there would be a deer tied down to the hood of one or two of the trucks. The sight of the deer carcass always filled me with a vague, dark ache: the perfect awfulness of the dead body.

"Coming up on the big day, little man," my father said the next morning at breakfast.

"Yes sir," I said, quietly.

He frowned a moment, drank the last of his coffee in a long swallow, smacked his lips, and got up to leave.

"Is everything okay?" he asked. He leaned over the back of his chair, propped on his long, solid arms. The butt of his revolver stuck out from the wide leather holster wrapped around his waist.

"Oh, sure," I said, and shrugged.

"Great," he said, his voice flat, his face creased as he peered down at me.

"Well," he said, and then smiled and ruffled my hair with his large strong hand, and kissed my mother, and left.

"Thomas," my mother said quietly. "Come on now. You've been gloomy for weeks, and now you're never home. What is it? Is it something at school?" She reached over and squeezed my cheek between her thumb and forefinger. "Come o-o-o-on, you're driving me crazy."

I hated it when she did that, but I couldn't help but grin as I pulled myself away.

"Do you think . . ." I began, and hesitated.

"Sometimes I do," she said, "if I'm not too busy."

I rolled my eyes. "Do you think Dad would be really upset, I mean if . . . I mean I'm supposed to go hunting with him, I know it's this big thing, this tradition, but . . ."

"Oh, Tommy, what? Just say it."

"I was thinking, what if I didn't want to? If I just didn't want to go?"

"But that's okay," she said quickly. "You don't have to. Oh baby, Dad thinks you want to go. It used to be all you'd ever talk about."

My mother was right about that. Just the year before, all I wanted in the world was a gun of my own. So much had happened to me in the past few weeks; when I was eleven going on twelve I couldn't see how parents might see time differently, might notice some things in their children, remember some things, and never see the changes as they came.

"I don't know," I said, and shrugged.

"If you want," she said, "I could tell him."

"No," I said quickly, and I wasn't at all sure why. "No, I was just thinking."

It was cold and overcast that day, a bleak, early winter day that suggested snow ahead, short nights, hot chocolate, and days spent hunting.

I walked slowly out through the woods, to find Emma.

"I can't spend as much time with you, Thomas," Emma told me, after we had walked a while. "Hunting season's coming. I need my rest. Anyway, I have some things I need to do."

"Things?" I cried, surprising her, I imagine, by how upset I suddenly was. "What things?"

"Oh, the world," she said, "things. I live in this little motor court and they're painting all the cottages this week. Heaven knows it's overdue, but I have to move some furniture about. And then my granddaughter is coming up from North Carolina . . ."

She shook her head. I stared at her. Even though she had told me about her family, it still hadn't really occurred to me that she lived somewhere, that she would ever have anything to do except walk these woods.

"You have a granddaughter? How old is she?"

She blew out a breath. "She's, what is she, twenty-six now? She doesn't know about me, about all this.

You know, Thomas, people think I'm just a little bit odd. She wants me to move down near her."

"Move?" I think I almost shouted this question.

"Oh, there's no question of my moving. No question. There's more I have to tell you; you know so little, yet. What I do here is tied to the land, to where I am. I couldn't move, not now. But I can't explain that to her."

I could see that she was unhappy, that whatever problems she had with her granddaughter were bothering her. All the same, I was feeling jealous and irritable. I didn't want her to have a family, or a cottage. I wanted her to walk with me, and teach me things.

"So, I'll be a little busy," she said, wearily.

"Okay," I said. I looked over at her. I wasn't sure, but I thought she might be crying. It was cold, and my eyes were watering a little.

"Emma?" I asked.

"The world is so vast, Thomas," she said abruptly. I was certain she was crying. She began to walk, and I scrambled up after her. She walked along, slowly, painfully it seemed. "You can't pick and choose what you want in it: the world comes all in a bunch. You should love what you can and," she drew in a long breath, "oh me, and try not to hate anything. Please believe me. Sometimes it gets away from me. I wish you could have met Mr. Nash. I don't set a very good example."

"Well, but, sure you do," I protested, "I don't understand!"

"Oh, don't mind me. I'm just getting old, Thomas."

"But you said Mr. Nash was a hundred and two!" I protested.

"Well, Mr. Nash didn't have a husband, and a store to run, and three children to raise." She shook her head. She was almost smiling now.

"No, he was a wonderful man. I've been Emma for so long . . ."

"What do you mean?"

"Hmm? What do I mean? Oh, very little, I assure you. I'm just tired. Weary, is the word. I'm just an old country woman, Thomas, old and worn out."

There was almost a lilt in her voice now.

"No," I said, and punched at her arm.

"Hmmph," she took another deep breath and smiled a rare, full smile. "Listen to me! What a sour old goat. Shouldn't all the world feel sorry for me!" She laughed now, a sound I loved to hear.

"You know," she said, "I must give you your birthday present a little early."

"Really?" I said, excited. I certainly hadn't expected a present from her.

"Yes. There's someone I'd like you to meet, before hunting season begins. A few someones. Can you meet me here early tomorrow? We have a long walk."

"Oh sure! Right after breakfast."

"Good," she said. "Good. Bring a little something to eat. And don't mind all my talk."

That evening I stood in the doorway of my parents' bedroom. My father had called across the house for me. He was sitting at the end of the bed untying his heavy black work shoes, to change into his slippers.

"Dad?" I said.

"Hey, sport," he said.

He looked at me, and for a moment nothing was said. He looked like he'd done something wrong, but he couldn't remember what. He looked at me like he couldn't quite place me. When he spoke he spoke slowly.

"Tom, about your birthday, you know." He took a breath, almost a sigh. "I mean, hey, we could always make some other plans."

"Mom told you."

"Ah, well, you know, she was worried about you. And maybe I haven't been paying enough attention lately, with work and all. But Tom, I thought you wanted to go with us."

He looked at me, searching my face. I didn't say anything. He shrugged.

"It doesn't matter," he said. "If you don't want to go hunting, then of course that's fine."

It was the strangest moment for me. For perhaps the first time I could see my father from a little distance, somehow. He was nervous. He wasn't sure what to say. I was amazed, and I hurt, with guilt and with what might have been a kind of fear.

"No, Dad," I said, my own voice sounding odd to me. "I was only thinking . . . I'm just not sure I could kill something, you know, a deer, a buck. I'm not sure."

"Oh, well, half the time you don't even get a decent shot at anything," he said, and chuckled. But then he looked up at me again. "Tom, I don't know if it will help, but when I shot my first deer . . ." He leaned his head back, and smiled from a long ago memory. "It was, let's see, the third time my dad took me hunting, and I remember I shot a small buck, just barely legal; and Tom, you see, I cried that night in bed. Okay? I mean, you don't have to spread it around, tell everyone, but I cried."

I stood there, four feet away, unable to breathe.

"Anyway, I did," he said, the words coming quickly now. "I mean, that's all. Does that help any?"

I nodded. "Thanks," I said. I was too scared to cry.

"Ah, c'mere," my father said and grabbed me in a quick hug. He ruffled my hair, turned me around, swatted me on my butt, and sent me on my way, more confused than I had ever been in my life.

Chapter 4

Early Saturday morning I dressed in a hurry and slipped quietly into my chair at the breakfast table. I know my parents thought there was something wrong. Breakfast was unusually quiet. My mother and father stole glances at each other, as I ate in hurried silence. I headed out the laundry door to the back deck, the yard, and the fields beyond, but not before I heard my mother's quiet comment to my father: "poor guy."

For all the turmoil I was going through, I was still excited about the prospect of a birthday present from Emma. I felt certain that a gift from her would be something magical. Though I had spent many long hours with her since that first day, walking and talking and exploring, the only real marvels I had seen were those at the very beginning: the deer, and the cuts and scratches on my face. Occasionally she would tell me about something she did. Once she found a doe, hung up in a barbed wire fence; it took her quite a while to get the deer untangled.

"And then?" I had asked her.

"Then I just shooed her away," Emma said.

"But was she hurt?"

"A little. Nothing much to worry her. She was more afraid of the fence, confused by being caught, than hurt."

"But you healed her?"

"I helped her a bit, yes."

That was as much as I could get from her that day. I hungered for the kind of wonders I had seen the first afternoon Emma and I met. I wanted my birthday present to be something amazing. It was.

"Where are we going?" I asked, breathless from running most of the way to our meeting place.

"Would you like to see where I live?" she asked in return. "There's someone there I'd like you to meet."

"Um, sure," I said, a little hesitantly, thinking, in the back of my mind, that probably my present was back at her cabin. Maybe it was too big to bring. I couldn't imagine what it would be.

It was a long walk to her place. I hadn't realized how far away she lived. She seemed happier than the she had been the day before, and stronger. It was a cold, clear morning; the walking warmed us quickly. I felt happier too, now that we were walking, and less expectant about a possible present, about anything. I had stowed away a few biscuits from breakfast, and Emma and I ate them early on. We fell in side by side, and for a long time neither of us spoke. I was enjoying the silence, and her company.

After a while, though, she began to talk. She seemed to be in a mood to teach again, which was fine with me.

As we walked she taught me more about deer, about their families. She told me how a young, strong buck might have two, three, or even more does as his mates. The deer traveled in small groups of perhaps six, ten, maybe twelve, that were a sort of loose family: the dominant buck, his does, a few young fawns, perhaps a weaker, submissive buck.

She said that the bucks fought for supremacy. They clashed with their heads lowered in charge, the violence of the collision sometimes so great as to snap their antlers. I could picture it; I slammed my hands together. She said that these battles, though, were usually tests of strength and will. The buck who lost was seldom seriously injured; he simply assumed a lower, submissive role in the family, or went to look for mates and supremacy elsewhere. When the deer battled in earnest, she told me, against wild dogs for instance, they lashed out with their front hooves, which are deadly sharp.

Emma said that the young fawns matured in a year or so, and might stay with the family or wander off to join another. Sometimes a young deer would rejoin its family after months, or even years, apart.

She said most bucks only lived to be two or three years old, they were hunted so. Her face tightened only a little as she told me this. She shook her head, seemed to force herself to cheer up.

"Do you know that deer can run as fast as forty miles an hour?" she said, her voice bright again with enthusiasm.

Well, no, I didn't know, but I was learning.

She nodded, emphatic and proud and happy. "They can. Did you know that they can leap between the wires of a barbed wire fence, say a foot apart," she showed with her hands, "at a full run, and not even brush the wires? I've seen it."

She spoke quickly and eagerly. I remember she seemed increasingly on edge, her cheerfulness forced, her teaching more mechanical, almost so that it began to seem eerie, unsettling.

We walked on, mile after mile. The cold, crisp air made for good walking weather. I felt happy and strong, but it seemed to me that Emma's moods were shifting quickly—cheerful for a few moments, and then tense, and sometimes just tired.

"I didn't know you had to walk so far to meet me," I said at one point. Emma's changeable mood was starting to make me edgy.

"These are all my woods, Thomas," she said. "I walk all through here, every day. It doesn't seem that far."

She gave me a brief, warm smile. It made me feel that I could ask a question I had been wondering about.

"What did you mean when you said that you couldn't leave here?"

"Hmm?" She seemed distracted.

"You said you were tied to the land, that you couldn't move away."

She stopped, took a deep breath. We had been walking at a brisk pace.

"Come here, Thomas," she said, and she knelt down.

I stepped over and knelt down too.

"Put your hand on the earth," she said. She had placed her hand firmly, palm down on the ground, so I did likewise. "What do you feel?"

"It's cold," I said, without really thinking. I looked into her eyes, a blue so bright it almost hurt. She was looking at me with such intensity that it frightened me.

"No, Thomas, it isn't," she said at last, with sorrow in her voice, and pitched herself awkwardly to her feet.

I got up and scrambled after her. There was something going on in her mind, and I didn't have a clue what it was.

"Emma," I said.

"Perhaps you are too young," she said quietly.

"I can't help how old I am," I said, rather curtly.

"Oh, Thomas, it's all right," she said, and she even gave a quick, rough laugh, at her own expense it seemed. "There are so many things I want to tell you about, and have you see, but you can't take everything in all at once and on the first try, now can you?"

"I don't know," I said.

Still smiling, she said, "Don't pay any attention to me."

We were nearing a roadway. For a little while I had been able to hear the occasional car go by. I was sulking a little. I didn't know what it was I was supposed to have felt or said back there, with my hand flat on the ground. It had felt cold to me.

All at once we were there. Just by the edge of the road was an old motor court, a winding crescent of small cottages tucked back in the trees. Emma took me firmly by the hand as we crossed the roadway. I remember that because it annoyed me. I was perfectly capable of crossing a road by myself, but I was too interested to see where she lived to be annoyed for long. The place gave the impression of age, but the cabins and grounds seemed well maintained. There was a gravel parking lot on the side of a big cabin that had a small hand-painted sign above the door: "Sleepy Hollow Motor Lodge." A wide, moss-covered brick pathway led back to a dozen or so small cabins. Emma's was the last cabin on the end.

An old dog limped over to us as we came up to her door.

"Hello, Abigail," Emma said warmly. "Ready for your treatment?"

Abigail's tail swished back and forth and up and down, the most lively part about her, it seemed. She looked to be terribly old.

"Is this your dog?" I asked.

"No, no. As much time as I spend away, I can't keep a dog," Emma said. "Abigail lives with the woman who runs this place, a few doors down. But we're old friends."

"What's her treatment?"

"She has an arthritic hip," Emma said, rubbing Abigail's side, "don't you, old girl?"

Abigail wagged her tail in agreement.

I frowned. "Well, can't you just, you know, fix it?"

Emma smiled. "Let's go inside," she said.

We entered her little cabin. There was one large room that served as living room, dining room, and kitchen. A short hallway lead back to a bedroom and bathroom. The main room was not cluttered, but it was not sparse, either. There was a small sofa, an easy chair, a bookcase full of books, a little coffee table with pictures on it. There was nothing especially modern in the room; she didn't have a television or a radio that I could see. The room looked plain, homey. It seemed odd to me, almost, how unremarkable the cabin was. I thought of Emma as being magical. I don't know if I expected a palace or a cave or what. I looked over at her and frowned. She was petting Abigail.

"I mean, can't you just make her hip better?" I said again.

"I can make it better," Emma said, "but I can't make it well. It's part of life that a body ages and doesn't hold up as well. Abigail's sixteen. She's entitled to a little arthritis."

"Sixteen is pretty old for dog, isn't it?" I asked.

Emma nodded, but didn't speak. She wasn't so much petting Abigail now, as running her hands slowly, lightly over Abigail's coat.

"Now listen closely, Thomas," Emma said quietly, and I stepped a bit closer. "Each particular body is different, and so is each part of each body. Are you listening?"

"Yes ma'am," I said. I called her ma'am sometimes now just to annoy her. A smile passed across her face for the briefest moment.

"It's important for you to understand that Abigail's hip is different from my hip, from yours, from a deer's, from another dog's hip, even one of the same size or breed. Her hip is hers. Do you understand?"

I nodded.

"Good," she said. "Each part of a body, of your body, and mine, and Abigail's, has, oh, a rhythm, or frequency, a pattern . . . I don't know how to say it, exactly. It has a right way for it to be, which you can sense, but, Thomas, you have to—Abigail, honey, now—" Abigail had become very still and was leaning, leaning into Emma such that she was about to topple over if Emma didn't hold her up. Emma pushed her upright and gave her a couple of little whacks on the fanny. Abigail's tail started wagging again.

"You have to be very clear, and empty," she said, looking at me closely to see if I was understanding her.

"Empty," I repeated, uncertain of what she meant.

"I don't know how to teach you this," Emma said. "Come here. Put your hand here."

I placed my hand on Abigail's back, and, with Emma's hand on top of mine, we gently stroked down the length of her coat.

"Each individual's body is unique," Emma said quietly. "Unique, precious, the only one in the universe.

You have to understand that; you have to accept it. Do you understand?"

She looked at me. We were still stroking the dog together.

"Not really," I said. I had to be honest.

"That's all right, Thomas. Dear Thomas. I'm sorry if I was cross with you earlier."

"That's okay," I said. I suddenly became very intent on stroking the dog. Then Emma's free hand rested lightly on the back of my neck. What happened next was so astonishing. It was the most incredible thing that had ever happened to me, short of being born, I guess. I suddenly had, felt, saw—a new sense. It's difficult to describe that moment. It was like being given the gift of sight after having always been blind. How would that be? I don't know. But I think I do know.

I could feel, in my gut, in a confused rush of sense and nonsense, the being of Abigail, her structure, her presence. Words fail. It was like seeing her in my heart. I looked over at Emma, but she had her eyes closed, as if she were concentrating fiercely. Her hand rested on top of mine. My neck felt on fire. I sprang away from them, Emma and Abigail, and rolled backwards and bumped into her coffee table and just crouched there in an odd bundle on her living room floor. After what seemed an eternity she opened her eyes.

"Are you all right?" she asked.

I nodded.

"Do you want to try that again?" she asked.

Again I nodded, more slowly this time, and crawled

back over to them. Abigail was again quite still, almost in a trance it seemed, leaning against Emma's leg. I carefully put my hand upon her back left hip—I knew now that her greatest pain was there—and Emma's hand rested lightly on mine, and then her other hand gently touched my neck.

"It's like there are two images," Emma whispered. "The one that is there and the one that should be there. But you have to be very careful. The one that should be there belongs to Abigail, exclusively to Abigail, not to you. It's not what you think should be there, but what truly should be there for Abigail. Can you feel it?"

I shook my head. "I don't know," I said. I thought of getting a television picture to come in correctly, adjusting the tuning knob. I could feel Abigail stiffen under my touch. I felt that the image I wanted was just out of reach, somehow. I pressed, or tried harder; it is so difficult to explain clearly. Suddenly Abigail whimpered, and then shuddered with pain. Her pain rolled through me in waves. I pushed myself away from her.

"You have to be gentle," Emma whispered sharply, her eyes tightly closed. "You have to be extremely careful. There's so much power in you, Thomas. You have to treat it with a tremendous respect."

"I don't want to hurt her," I said.

"I know. Tell her it's okay. You tell her."

"I'm sorry, Abigail," I said. I was near to crying. "I'm sorry."

Abigail pushed herself against me again, but I was reluctant to touch her.

"I don't know if I can do this," I said.

"Let's rest a minute," Emma said. She looked suddenly, deeply tired.

I lay back flat on the floor and stared up at the ceiling. That second time, feeling, knowing Abigail's hip, had been much clearer for me. I had hurt her, though. There was pain there to begin with, but I had made it worse. It was unsettling to be confronted with such a new, and frightening, power. It frightened me to feel responsible for Abigail's well being, to know I could help her, but not know how or why I could help. For the briefest moment I had felt that I could have, quite accidentally, crushed her hip, her body, the way one might sneeze or hiccup without meaning to.

"You have to be clear," Emma said, her quiet voice suddenly filling the room. "I wish I could think of a better way to explain it."

"Clear," I said back to her, my voice flat.

"No expectations," Emma said. "Not even so much as the wish to help her." She paused, reconsidered. "I mean, of course you want to help her."

I rolled my head over with what seemed great effort to look at Emma. She was looking at me. Just then Abigail let out a great, big sigh, as if she were somewhat exasperated with us both. Emma chuckled.

"You want to help her but your intention should be, should only be, that she be more properly herself, more perfectly herself. You're not fixing Abigail's hip, but, somehow, giving her hip back to her, the way it should properly be. Do you see that at all?"

"I think so, maybe."

"Tell me."

I frowned. "Well, it's her hip. It's not mine to give."

"Yes, Thomas. Yes, that's right."

"And it's like you said, she's old, she has an old hip. But she doesn't need to have that much pain."

I was still looking over at Emma. Her eyes were shining.

"Let me try again," I said.

"Carefully," she said.

This time I felt calmer. What I was trying to do, with Emma's help (she never let go of either my hand or my neck), was to lead Abigail this minuscule distance. It was as if her hip was just the slightest bit out of alignment, and I was trying to nudge it back into place, with my heart, through my hands. It's hard to describe it any better than that. It was clear to me at the time. I sensed that there was a place or a state where her hip was supposed to be, and if I could just nudge it a little part of the way it would fall into place of its own accord. And it did.

I blinked, and sat back again. I pushed Abigail away from me. Her tail started wagging again, with enthusiasm. She was glad it was over; she felt better. She nuzzled my hand with her head and I patted her a few times but then I pushed her away again. In a funny way I had suddenly had quite enough of her. My hands felt hot. I realized I was sweating: my forehead and chest were hot and moist.

"Okay," I said, to Abigail, who was pushing against me again. "Go somewhere."

I was tired. I was very, very tired. Emma climbed to her feet and more or less dragged Abigail out of the cabin. Then Emma came back and all but collapsed on the sofa. She patted the cushion next to her.

"Come," she said.

I climbed up from the floor onto the cushion, and leaned heavily against her. I felt like I could sleep for hours.

"Is it always that hard?" I asked.

"You get used to it," she said weakly, and then chuckled again. This day was the warmest, the kindest she had been with me. I loved seeing her smile, hearing her small, rough laugh. "I never showed anyone before. It's hard work."

"Thank you," I said.

"Hmm," was all she said. "There is more for your birthday, but let's rest a while first."

"More? There can't be more."

"There's more."

I wriggled into a more relaxed position. She draped her arm across me, a bit awkwardly at first, but then more tenderly. I never thought to ask if she was comfortable. We sat that way, I don't know how long, not talking, just resting. I felt like I could have stayed there forever, just like that. I closed my eyes.

After a time, she asked: "Are you sleeping?"

"Yes," I said.

"Good," she answered. "I need to tell you some things. None of this is quite right, but it's the best I can tell you. Now, there's a basic goodness at the heart of things, Thomas. A basic, clear, simple goodness in every stone and tree and animal—in everything. It's not something that you can see or that someone can prove to you. But it's there. And it's not a human goodness, it's not nice, or fair, or comfortable; there are terrible things in the world, more terrible even than you or I can imagine. But through it all, at the deepest core, is this simple, basic goodness. You have to believe that. You have to find it in your heart to believe that. Are you listening to me?"

I was very still, lying against her. I breathed when she breathed.

"No," I said.

"Good, that's good." She kissed me lightly on the top of the head. "Here's the tricky part, maybe. Everything has its own simple goodness. It's not just the same, everywhere, one big bland good thing. Each thing, each creature has its own particular good heart, which is unique, different from all the rest. You have to believe and respect and cherish each one. It's hard, sometimes. I mean, sometimes it's basically impossible. But you have to try. Nothing I've taught you means anything if you don't try. And the first heart, the most important heart to cherish, is your own. That's what I meant about being clear. You have to clear everything out until there is just this good, simple Thomas left."

As she finished talking I found that I had begun to cry. I was thinking of my father, and my birthday, and everything that was supposed to happen on that day. I knew, resting there with Emma, that I could never hunt, could never shoot an animal, but how could I tell my father that? I felt dread, and shame. I felt dishonest for not telling Emma what was going on. I felt anything but clear, anything but simple or good.

For all that I was tired. Abigail had drained me somehow. I felt sad, and very unsure of myself. Emma was there, supporting me, warm. I fell asleep.

I don't know if I slept for five minutes or an hour and half. I woke to the sound of voices, to a quiet but definite argument. I was curled up, alone on the sofa. I didn't move or open my eyes.

"He's too young," I heard a man's voice say. The voice was old but its timbre was rich and strong.

"He's young," Emma said.

"Too young."

"What is too young? How do you know? He's sweet and gentle and he has the quiet. You've seen him in the woods. He's gifted in our way."

"That's as may be. But he hasn't lived. You can't put this on him so early, before he's had some stretch of life. You and I were well along before we started in earnest. Those years are a great help."

"I know," Emma said. She was silent a few moments. "I care for him. I want to give him this."

"Wait a while. A long while."

"I don't know how long I've got. I'm not a young woman, you know." There was a light humor in her voice.

"You have time, I'm sure of it. Lots of time. And so does he. You can't pull a sapling up by the roots to help it grow."

"I know that," Emma said, a little sharply. "I know that."

"Work with him, but patiently. Think years. Let him grow away from you and come back."

"Oh, Mr. Nash, I don't want him to grow away."

Mr. Nash. I sat up from the couch, quickly, and my head swam a moment, and there was Emma, alone, staring out the front window of her cabin. She looked down at me.

"Oh, hello," she said.

"I heard . . ." I looked around; there was no one in the cabin but us. "I heard you talking."

"I'm sorry," she said quietly. "I didn't mean to wake you."

I just sat there, my head cloudy, looking at her, and she looked back at me, her face blank, flat, and then she smiled a little sadly. I felt, at that moment, that I had lost something, that she was pulling away from me.

"I'm not too young," I said.

"Come on," Emma said, as if I had not spoken. "It's getting late and we have another little walk ahead of us."

All of the sudden everything was normal between us, or was supposed to be. Emma walked over to the little kitchenette and started putting together sandwiches for us. She poured me a glass of milk and gave me a couple of chocolate chip cookies.

"I guess I should have baked you a cake," she said.

"Naw," I said. "Anyway, my birthday's not for a while yet."

"I know," she said quietly. She packed a bag with some small apples that looked a little mushy to me. I wasn't so sure I was going to want any of those. But my sandwich was good, and I gobbled down my cookies and drank my milk. I was hungry, sleepy, sad. There were too many things going on for my young head and heart to sort out. Emma was a little distant from me, and I just had to let that be. I didn't have anything like the power or energy to bridge the gap between us.

Outside the cabin, I gave Abigail a farewell pat. It was odd, petting her. I could feel nothing, now. She was just a cheerful old dog. It was hard for me to remember what that feeling, so intense at the time, had been like. I felt like I had lost something, lost it before I had ever really had it.

I was feeling quiet and subdued, then, as we plunged back into the old forest that bordered the highway, I realized, vaguely, that we were headed back toward my home, but not directly. Anyway, we were still miles away.

"Where are we?" I asked Emma.

"Up near Harrow Point. That was Highway 12, you know, where I live. We don't have far to go, just a mile or so."

We walked on in silence. It felt good to be out in the woods again. This was something I was used to. I started to feel a little more like myself, to feel less the wonder and strangeness of what had happened in Emma's cabin.

"Okay," she said. "We're almost there. A little more quietly, now."

We were at the edge of a large natural pasture, ringed with trees, covered with tall grass and low shrubs and bushes. We crept forward. An orange and black monarch butterfly batted along in the bright sunshine.

"Hello-o-o!" Emma called softly.

I could see nothing. We waited. It seemed impossible to me that the air could be so still. Then, from behind a clump of bushes some twenty yards away, walked a large, beautiful, reddish-brown doe, her head held high, sniffing the air. As I smiled with delight, Emma's hand came up and rather snugly squeezed the back of my neck.

"So you can hear," she whispered.

"What?" I asked, and then I did hear, or felt, or saw, smelt a soft, thick, mumbly voice.

"Danger? Danger?" it said.

"It's me," Emma said. "You remember. I've brought someone."

"Danger?" the voice asked, and I realized in a breathless flash that I was hearing the doe.

Or not hearing. It was the strangest thing: another new sense, similar, adjacent to the other I had experienced that day. It was not that I was hearing the doe, but that I knew or felt something from her that came to me as words, thin and high, that flowed from the deer and echoed, clear and simple and strange, somewhere in my chest.

"I wouldn't bring you danger," Emma said. Her voice was quite ordinary and direct, like she was speaking to a friend who was just a bit hard of hearing.

"You bring strength," came the reply; and then, "What is it? What is it?"

"A boy, a man-child. He is not danger."

The doe walked forward in halting, uncertain steps, looking always as if she were just about to flee. With each step she stamped at the ground with her forelegs.

"She's letting the others know that someone's here," Emma said. "They can hear and feel it when she stamps like that."

"Wowwww," was all I could think to say.

The doe's nose twitched nervously as she stood just six feet from us. She turned her head all the way to the left, eyeing me with care, then slowly turned her head all the way to the right, her eyes never leaving mine.

"Food?" she asked.

"Why yes," Emma said. "I brought some apples." She opened the sack she had been carrying and showed the food inside to the doe. "I brought them for you, and for the family, and for Reggie."

She said the name slowly, as if it held some significance, and in a moment the deer had bolted away to the far side of the pasture, and into the trees. Emma relaxed the grip on my neck.

"Ahh," I said, disappointed, thinking we had lost her.

"Who's Reggie?" I asked.

"Her buck," Emma answered. "He's the king of these woods, in his way. I named him Reggie."

I drew my breath in sharply. From across the meadow I saw the largest deer I had ever seen. A huge, majestic buck with a vast rack of antlers stepped slowly from the edge of the trees, and seemed to drift, rather than walk, toward us.

"He scarcely needs a fool like me to give him a name," Emma said quietly.

He seemed the pure embodiment of strength and stately grace. In spite of myself, of Emma, of everything, I thought: "God, what a trophy." His antlers, I meant: an incredible prize for a hunter. I shook the thought away angrily.

"Emma," I said urgently, suddenly desperate to confess to her that I was supposed to go hunting in little more than a week.

"Shhh," she said. "He's coming."

He progressed firmly but slowly across the pasture. Behind him came six more deer: three does, a little button buck, a small fawn, and a small adult buck. These six wove along through the grass and brush, now stopping, now starting again, raising their noses high, sniffing the wind. Twice the little fawn burst back toward the safety of the trees, only to gallop up again to the rear of the slowly advancing group. Emma repeated her grip on the back of my neck.

"Strength," said a deep, rumbling voice that filled my body. I knew it must be Reggie.

"Strength," said Emma, and nodded her head slightly. She let go of my neck a moment and batted me lightly on the back of my head.

"Strength," I said, uncertainly.

"How is your family?" asked Emma, as she rested her hand on the back of my neck once again.

"One is weak," said the buck.

"I will see to them all," said Emma. "I have brought a man-child to meet you."

Reggie looked me over slowly, the way the first doe had, turning his head slowly first to one side, then to the other.

"Man-child," he rumbled.

"Sir," I said, in awe of his size and bearing, of the breadth and development of his antlers, which arched high above his powerful head and neck.

"No danger," Reggie said.

At that the other deer walked toward me with a little less timidity, their ears high and wide, all sniffing like mad, making these loud snorting sounds. The little fawn hid behind the three does, and would not approach. The button buck took a step forward, a step back, then danced forward and butted me once, quite sharply, in the stomach.

"Hey!" I said, and laughed.

He butted me again, and I rapped him on the top of his head, between the small buds which would one day be antlers. He scampered off, and scampered back, feinting and dodging like a boxer.

"He likes you," Emma said.

"Sure," I said, beaming. I reached out and tried to tap his head again; he dodged and butted me a good one on the side of my leg.

"Walk," Reggie said suddenly, and began to walk away from us, back to the center of the meadow.

"Here," said Emma, "he means you." She closed her

eyes, touched my neck, and I felt a sudden burst of electricity course through me, from her hand into my neck and down through my toes.

"Oww!" I cried.

"I didn't hurt you," said Emma a bit tersely, and pushed me toward Reggie. I walked out toward him, confused and more than a little scared.

"Speak simply and honestly," Emma said. "Above all, honestly. He'll understand you, in his way, if what you say comes from your heart."

"Man-child," he said again.

"Oh!" I exclaimed, and turned back toward Emma. I could hear him on my own. She simply waved me away, and turned to begin examining the other deer, laying her hands on their coats, rubbing them gently. I walked toward Reggie, looking back toward Emma.

"She gives strength," Reggie said. "What do you give?"

"I, uh, well, nothing, sir," I said. "I guess."

"You are family?"

"No," I said. "We're friends. She teaches me."

"You give strength," he said.

"No," I said. "No, I . . ."

"You give strength," he said.

We walked a while in silence. Reggie walked very slowly, the muscles of his flanks rippling with controlled power. He made me feel frightened and sad at the same time.

"What will you do when the hunters come?" I asked, my voice trembling.

The answer came in words that formed in me, slowly, distinctly.

"What we always do. Hide. Move from the meadows up to the hills. Watch for the men. Stay still and let them pass. Follow, watch, and hide."

"Follow?"

"Follow," Reggie said, the voice that formed within me was flat, emotionless. "The men walk and walk and walk. We follow and watch. It is safe."

"Are you . . . are you afraid?"

"Some will die," he said. "Always, some will die. I am old, but I am strong. I will survive."

We walked back to Emma and the other deer.

"When do the men come?" asked Reggie.

"Nine days," Emma said.

I heard the single word "danger" echo among the different voices.

"Strength will be with us?" Reggie asked.

"I'll be here," Emma said.

Emma and I walked slowly southward, the sun casting enormous shadows from our right. The meadow where we met Reggie and the other deer was a good two-hour walk from the woods near my home, from the places I was familiar with. It seemed that by unspoken agreement Emma would walk me most of the way home.

We didn't speak for a long time. The air was cool. The terrain rolled and dipped. We would descend into a slight hollow and lose the sun altogether, entering spaces where the air was so cold it seemed no warmth could have reached there since late last fall. Then up into the warmer, brighter air, and we would walk across long stretches of fairly level ground that appeared to surround us for miles on all sides. Then we would find ourselves descending again into another dark, cool swale.

I felt older. I felt that I had aged years that day, that I had learned and seen and heard more in that day than in the rest of my life put together. I felt like the day had changed me, permanently. But there was still so much that I didn't understand.

I could hear Emma's breathing as she walked along beside me, now slightly ahead, now slightly behind. On rare occasions her age betrayed her; she had had a long day, and her breathing was loud, almost labored.

"I heard you talking in the cabin," I said, a note of challenge in my voice that I hadn't really intended.

Emma did not respond.

"When I was sleeping, I heard you talking to Mr. Nash," I said.

"When you were sleeping," Emma said finally, letting the words hang a moment.

"I heard you talking to Mr. Nash," I said more forcefully.

Emma shook her head. "I can't tell you everything all at once," she said. "We've had a big day as it is, don't you think?"

There was no answering that.

We kept walking. I was getting tired, and a feeling of

irritation loomed deep in me. Emma was teaching me and showing me so much, and yet she was holding back from me as well. It was like being given short glimpses of a great and wondrous sight. I wanted to see; I wanted to see the whole thing and understand.

"I'm not too young," I said again, as if picking up a conversation from hours ago.

"Yes you are," Emma said, and then did something she had not done in all our walks together. She took my hand.

She was slowing me down. We were passing over a bit of low outcropping rock, as appears now and again in these woods, and her hand passed up to my arm, and I realized, with something of a shock, that she was leaning on me. I picked our way along, self-consciously slow, looking for places where we could both walk securely. The area was small, and soon we were back on level ground, walking between the high, silent trees, the sun sinking. Emma's hand dropped into mine, and then let go, and then we were walking along again, side by side, in the evening air that was now decidedly cold.

"Isn't this a beautiful time of day?" Emma said. "Isn't this a rare and beautiful thing?"

"Yes, ma'am," I said quietly, not meaning to needle her, but feeling strange and blue.

"Thomas," she said. "I should apologize to you, but I won't. I've been trying to fill your head and your heart with so many new things and you've tried so manfully to absorb it all."

"I like it when you teach me," I said.

"I know you do. I like it too. But sometimes I should be quiet more and just let us walk. There is nothing greater than deep and simple gratitude at being in such a beautiful place. There's nothing that I can teach you that is greater than this moment."

She had stopped walking. I went on ahead a few paces, and turned when I realized she wasn't coming.

"Look," she said firmly.

We were at the top of a high, wide ridge. Below us was a small ravine that led gradually up into the woods that I knew. We were a mile or so from my home. The trees were thinner here, up top, affording the nearest thing to a panoramic view we could have in such a wooded area. The sun was a squat orange ball, low in a cobalt blue sky. Emma's face was aglow in the light of the setting sun. I don't think I was exactly getting it, that I was understanding what she had said. But perhaps I did, after all. For as long as I could remember I had loved the beauty of the woods, and the quiet.

"These are your woods," Emma said.

I nodded. We stood a while longer, just a minute or so, when the quiet of the evening was broken by a loud snapping sound. There were deer, four or five of them, walking along the bottom of the ravine. They might have been a hundred yards away—much farther than it seemed from the sound they made. I could just make them out as they moved among the trees.

"Wish them well," Emma said. "Try to hold them in your heart and wish them strength."

I looked at her a bit quizzically. I mean, it was not as if I would wish the deer ill. We watched in silence as they passed out of view. I put up a hand, as if to wave goodbye to them, which immediately felt like a foolish thing to do. We stood together, watching the woods where the deer had been. It felt to me that the day was over.

"Thank you for . . ." I shrugged. "For showing me stuff today," I said.

"You're welcome, dear," Emma said.

"So, you know," I began, feeling suddenly nervous, "will I see you after school this week?"

I already knew the answer.

Emma sighed, sounding somewhere between tired and exasperated.

"I have to rest," she said. "Let's say, the week after."

I frowned. The week after would be after my birthday. It seemed a long, long time away.

"I've been trying to cram you full of things all day," she said.

"That's okay," I interrupted.

" . . . so let me cram in just a little more. Thomas, what I showed you today, working with Abigail, it's not something you could learn, like learning anything; I don't know, like learning to play the piano. It's not a skill by itself. It's something . . ." she stopped, her hand gesturing vaguely. She looked at me, and chuckled.

"I'm not very good at explaining these things," she said with a wry smile.

"Just tell me," I said.

"It's part of a life, a way of living and seeing and

being that, well, it's different for everyone but it's not that different, really." She chuckled. "Now that makes sense, doesn't it?"

She was smiling. I shrugged.

She shook her head. "It's about intention," she said flatly. "You have to live your whole life around this intention to help, an intention to help and to heal. But it has to come from this simple and humble place. That's the difficult part, for me anyway. Everything you do has to help that intention. It can get away from you so easily, all the details and problems and nonsense that comes from being alive. Just this little nuisance of them painting my cabin—it's such a simple thing and such an aggravation. Somehow amid everything, all the distractions, you have to nurture this clear intention to help and gradually, gradually you grow into it. But Thomas, it's so hard to do. Believe me, it's hard, and you never, ever finish. You never quite get it right. But for the love of everything, the sake of everything, you can never stop trying. Every time you feel yourself failing, falling away from where you should be, you have to try to return to that clear, humble space, to live from there. Do you understand at all what I am saying?"

"I don't know," I said, or almost cried. She was asking too much of me.

Her voice dropped a notch. She stepped closer to me.

"Do one thing for me this week," she said.

"Okay," I answered, after she had stared at me hard a moment.

"Before you go to sleep tonight, I want you to imagine a circle around you, wish for a circle around you, and everything in that circle will be safe, and healthy, and strong."

"A circle," I repeated.

"It starts in your heart and comes out all around you, out of your fingertips and toes. Just imagine it. Wish that it was so, like make believe. This isn't hard, Thomas."

I think I was looking away from her.

"I'm listening," I said.

"Just pretend that within this circle everything is healthy and strong, wish that it would be so. Let the circle be small, just big enough to surround you and anything you might touch, and then, slowly, let the circle grow."

I was looking at her now.

"Let it become big enough to reach around your house, to hold your father and mother. Let the circle come back to you, and then cast it a little wider, out to the woods where you live, and then back, and cast it a little wider, a little farther each time. And Thomas, do this for me: cast your circle all the way out to me."

"I will," I said, but then I hesitated. "It won't—it won't do anything. It won't really help anything."

"You don't know that," Emma said firmly, but there was a light smile in her eyes. "Anyway, it's a wish. And it's good practice. So do it. Tell me you'll do it, each night."

"I will," I said again.

"And remember," she said, and now she was turning, and walking away from me. "Remember, the circle surrounds you, too. Be sure to include yourself, healthy and strong and well. And throw that last circle all the way out to me—don't forget, all the way to me, dear."

"I will," I said a final time, to her back, as she began her walk home. I thought I heard her say "That's good," but I wasn't sure. I wanted to call after her, to call her back, but I didn't. In just a few moments it was hard to see her in the falling dusk, and then she was gone altogether. It was strange, awful; I had the strongest sense that I would not see her again.

I was too old to cry, I thought. I was too old to run home crying. So I walked home, slowly, purposefully, thinking about Abigail, thinking about Emma, and Reggie, and wanting to send out a circle that would encompass them all, without being at all sure what that would mean.

Chapter 5

I tried, that first night, to do as Emma had told me, but almost as soon as I was in my bed I fell into a deep and dreamless sleep, with little more than vague thoughts, images in my mind of circles and balls flying and bouncing around my room. My mother practically had to pull me out of bed in the morning. All the events of the day before had left me feeling heavy and stupid. I don't think I was awake in any useful sense until I was at school, sitting at my desk, gradually aware of all the noise and chatter around me.

Hunting season was barely a week away. In such a rural community as ours, the beginning of deer season was a major occasion. It seemed like every boy in school was talking about who was going hunting this year for the first time, who had a gun of his own, and who didn't. I had been withdrawn somewhat from all this talk. But then, I had always been a fairly quiet person.

Among the boys at school I had a status of sorts, because my father was a policeman: to a bunch of eleven and twelve-year-old boys, being a policeman was about the greatest thing a man could be. If I was quiet, if I kept my thoughts to myself, it wasn't put down to being shy or awkward or overly introspective; in the odd, scarcely explicable world of schoolyard politics, I was Deputy Singer's son, and so I didn't need to be funny, or smart, or tough, or anything else. It was a blessing which, like all blessings I suppose, I could neither earn nor deserve, but had just been handed to me.

In truth, I didn't have anywhere near enough confidence to voice my newfound conviction that I wouldn't go hunting when the season began. There was no one I could talk to about Emma. I certainly wasn't going to tell my friends that I had been speaking with deer, and learning to heal an old, arthritic dog. If anyone among the boys at school had the least reservation about hunting, I never heard it. And they weren't going to hear it from me.

Indeed, my friends at school were certain that I was going to go hunting. My father had told me months before that he would take me hunting on my birthday. And for years my parents had said, in answer to my pestering and pleading, that I could have a shotgun of my own for my twelfth birthday, but not before. All this my friends knew, because I had told them.

So in the lunchroom that day it was natural that I would, after all, be drawn into the talk of hunting season.

"You going to the meeting tomorrow night?" Cady, one of my friends, asked me.

"Yeah," I said, "I have to help my dad with stuff."

"My dad says 'next year, maybe next year,'" Cady said, "but it's my mom that won't let me go."

I just nodded. There was a meeting for hunters at the firehouse the next night, and my father would be talking about hunting safety there. I was going.

"My dad told my mother I was going hunting whether she liked it or not," Mike said.

"If my dad said that to my mother, she would kick his ass," Cady said matter-of-factly.

We chuckled, but only a little. We all knew Cady's mom.

"I'm gonna find me a buck and BAM," Mike slammed his fist down on his tray with sufficient force to make his tater tots pop into the air, which pleased him enough that he slammed his fists in rapid succession. "BAM BAM BAM!"

Cady shook his head. "You saw a buck, you'd wet your pants."

"You can kiss my big ol' butt," Mike said companionably.

"My dad says you don't even see one, half the time," I said. "Don't even see a deer."

"Where are you all going to go?" Cady asked.

I shrugged.

"We're going out behind my grand-daddy's farm," Mike said. "There's all kind of land back there, and can't no one hunt it but family. I'm going to find me a buck, you watch."

"You want to bet?" Cady asked.

"Well," Mike said, "my father won't let me bet, or I would."

"Sure you would," Cady said, and then turned to me, and tapped his fork on the table top. "I wish I was going with you, wherever you all go."

"Probably won't be anything," I said quietly.

"Your dad will find some deer, you watch."

That evening my father came home early from work, which was rare. I had only been home from school for a half an hour or so, and was more or less moping around the house.

"Not going prowling in the woods this afternoon?" my mother had asked.

"Not today," I said. "I've got some stuff to do." Which was clearly not the case. Our little dog, Toby, was following me around from room to room. All at once I thought I felt the question 'play?' form inside me, and I swung around and looked at Toby, who was just standing there, staring at me. His tail flipped from one side to the other, and then he stood still.

"Come here," I said, and sat down on the floor.

Toby bounced over and pushed his head against my side, his tail wagging, ready for a bit of play.

"No," I said. "Hold still."

He was still interested in playing, but I managed to get him still, and then I slowly ran my right hand along the ridge of his small back, my eyes closed, trying to rediscover that other, strange, wonderful sense, trying to recreate what Emma had showed me to do with Abigail . . . but there was nothing there, just Toby's back, like always. I frowned. Toby began wagging his tail again. And then I heard my father's cruiser pulling into the drive.

I went over to the window and saw my father walking to the house with a couple of shotguns cradled in one arm and a box of shells in the other. I scrambled outside to help him.

"Hey, sport," he said, a smile spreading across his face. "Give me a hand, here?"

I immediately reached for the smaller of the two shotguns.

"You remember John McCumber?" my dad asked.

I nodded.

"This gun belongs to his wife; he ordered it special for her. I thought we might shoot a little before dinner, see if you like it."

I nodded again. The gun was a beauty. It had a good weight and balance to it. I wanted to shoot it. I can't explain the reason why. For all that had happened to me in the past weeks, I found the gun beautiful, enticing, and I wanted to shoot it.

We walked down to the field down behind the house. My father lugged down an old door that had been sitting in the shed, and I carried the shotguns and the shells. He leaned the door against a tree and we moved back thirty paces or so.

"Well, say we're going to shoot at this door," my father said.

"Guess we're not going to use it for anything," I said with a grin.

"Not if we manage to hit it," my father said, "but if we're going to shoot at it, what are we going to do first?"

I nodded. I knew what he was after. "Well, we want to check the guns, make sure they're clean, that the barrel is clean, and the shells are good."

"I've done that," my father said.

"Uh huh," I said, "but I'll check my gun anyway, 'cause you should always check your own gun."

My father nodded. I could tell from his eyes that he was pleased with me.

"And there's nothing down there behind that tree; the house and all is behind us and there's nothing down there, but we might walk down and see, you know."

"There's nothing down there," my father said.

"And I know where you are, you know, my shooting partner. There's nobody else with us."

"Good," my father said. "That's fine. Well, let's see if this thing'll shoot."

"Yes sir," I said.

I cracked the gun open, sighted down the barrel. It was beautifully clean and oiled, as I knew it would be. My father handed me a new shell. I popped it into the barrel, snapped the gun shut, placed the stock against my shoulder.

"Snug," my father said. He was standing beside me, and pressed the butt of the gun more tightly against my shoulder. "Good and snug, but not rigid. Brace it, but let it come back into you. It's going to pop you one, but just keep it snug and keep your eye and cheekbone up. Up. You don't want to get a black eye."

"Yes sir," I said.

He messed my hair. "Okay, step away," he said. "You're too tight."

Before this, I'd only shot a little .22 rifle, plinking at tin cans on the ground from time to time with my father. God, I really wanted to fire that shotgun and shoot it well. The feeling was so strong: a tight, edgy joy, like great avarice on the brink of being satisfied. Ten minutes before I had been sitting on the floor with Toby, trying to practice the skills Emma had taught me, with no idea my father would be bringing a shotgun home for me to shoot. Now I was acutely focused on aiming at that door and hitting it square with buckshot, without another thought in the world.

My father nodded at me. "Snug against your shoulder, cheek bone up, squeeze the trigger. Have at it."

A moment later there was a roar and a ripping sound of splintered wood. The door spun to the right—I had hit the right side of it—did a comically slow pirouette, and fell to the ground with a deeply satisfying "whuu-ump."

I laughed, my father laughed.

"Great shot," my father said, and I knew he meant it.

I rubbed my shoulder and said "Oww," and my father laughed again.

My father set the door up and we fired at it a few more times. By the time we finished there was nothing left of it recognizable as a door.

That night I went to bed with an ice pack on my shoulder. I had a sizable welt that would turn into a splendid bruise. I was happier than I could ever remember being. It was a door, after all, that we had been shooting at. No harm had been done. I thought for a moment of Emma, and believed that I could spread a circle of strength and well-being all the way to Mars.

My father came in then to check on me, and take the ice pack.

"You handled that gun real well," he said. "I'm proud of you."

"I was a pretty good shot," I said.

He nodded. "And you knew what to do beforehand, which is what's really important. I liked that you checked the gun, even after I told you it was okay."

"You told me always to check it myself," I said. "You told me that a bunch of times."

"Well, you listened," he said. "That shoulder going to keep you awake?"

"It'll be okay," I said.

"Good," he said. Up to now it had been my father's custom to give me a kiss goodnight, on the forehead. This night he hesitated, a look of what I knew was pride on his face. He gave my leg a couple of good, hard pats.

"Good night, Thomas," he said.

My shoulder was aching, but I soon fell into a deep and peaceful sleep.

Each year they had a big meeting of all the local hunters, or most of them at any rate, where you could buy a hunting license for the year if you didn't have one already, and where a deputy from the sheriff's department would go over any changes in the hunting laws and talk about safety issues. Very little of anything new was said at these meetings, but it gave the men an opportunity to get together each year and talk guns and hunting, argue about the best places to hunt, and tell tall tales about hunts from the years before.

For the past several years my father had given the safety talk to the hunters, and just the year before he let me come with him and help set up. There wasn't anything for me to do, really, except hand out some informational brochures the state had made up about hunting safety. I think my father just wanted me to be there. Certainly, the year before I had very much wanted to go. Now, the day after firing a shotgun that I knew would be like mine, I kept any reservations I had resolutely to one side. Nothing had been decided. It was just a meeting, a chance to see a bunch of people we knew, and I was glad to be going.

We pulled into the parking lot of the firehouse and I carried a big box full of safety brochures up toward the house, one step behind my father.

The fire station had a meeting hall upstairs in a large

room above the truck bay. I always loved going to the firehouse. If there was anything better in the world than being a sheriff's deputy, like my father, it might have been being a fireman and riding around in one of those fantastic big trucks. We walked past the open doors of the truck bay—my father didn't look at the trucks so I tried not to, as well—and on upstairs to the meeting hall.

It was a big meeting and there were men we knew all over the firehouse. Downstairs in the dispatch bay some guys were talking, and more men were clogging up the steps. Just ahead of us I heard someone, laughing, chiding, "Son, you're too big to stand there. Either go up or go down, but go somewhere." There was laughter. It was Roy Campbell talking to Mac Lewis, and Mac was a big man, sure enough, and he laughed and stayed right where he was, and we slid past him up the stairs, saying hello to everyone. Mac slapped me on the butt on my way by.

There were snatches of conversation, greetings called out. I heard Harmon Williams say, "Yeah, up to my little cabin, gonna sit with a little George Dickel an' my shotgun an' shoot anything that I see . . ." this being received with Andy Powell's high pitched laugh: "Gonna shoot anything you see!" Andy repeated. Tom Lamott saying quietly, intently to Lester Houchens, "Won't go to the doctor and I can't make her, you know?" and Lester nodding.

We moved through the crowd of men up towards the front of the meeting room. We knew everyone there. The county was only so large, my father had lived there all his life, and it was just a fact of life that everybody knew everybody else. Being somewhere like the firehouse, full of all these people we knew, was a good feeling, better than good: it felt like home, an extension of home. Maybe there were eighty men there, and I would say at one time or another they had all been to our house, and most had sat to dinner with us.

I remember when my Uncle Robert died, it seemed like everyone we knew came to our house that day, to be with my mom, to bring us food, or just to be there. And like any occasion when everyone would get together, people broke off into different groups, some talking quietly, and some not so quietly, and laughter here or there. I don't know, but every man at the meeting that night might have been at our house the day after Uncle Robert died. Maybe.

We got upstairs and my father gravitated over toward Richard Healy, the captain of the fire department, and a good friend of my dad's. Who all was there? Mitchell Cromer, Mike Powell, Merwin's brother (Merwin would be along eventually), and Andy Karl was there, with this godawful bad haircut, cut really close but splotchy with bits sticking out here and there.

"Hey, Tom," Mitchell said to me. "Come to help your Daddy?"

"Yes sir," I said, nodding to the box I was carrying.

"They got some Cokes back in the kitchen if you want," Mike said. "Can the boy have a Coke?" he asked my father.

My dad nodded. "If you want," he said to me.

I set the box down on the table up front and was about to go to the kitchen when Hally Lynch came over, his eyes big, grinning at Andy.

"Now what on earth got a hold of your head?" Hally asked Andy, checking out his haircut from a couple of angles.

My father doesn't like to laugh at people. When he doesn't want to laugh he just grins and his body shakes a bit. He started shaking now.

"Aw, Allison said she'd cut my hair . . ." Andy began, but Hally didn't let him finish.

"Was she drunk?" Hally asked, slow and loud, happy, relishing every word. "Did you all have a fight?"

Allison and Andy had only recently been married. Andy was blushing now, but he was still trying to keep his dignity.

"She said why pay Martin seven dollars for a haircut when she'd be happy to cut it for me," he tried to explain.

Hally was shaking his head, trying to look serious. "Son," he said, putting his hand on Andy's shoulder. "Pay the seven dollars. If it's a matter of money, I'm sure we can come up with a little for you."

"Well," Andy said, trying not to laugh, "you see . . ."

"Now I don't like to say anything bad about anybody's wife," Hally continued—there were a few people standing around us now, laughing—"and Allison is a fine lady; but, Andy, keep that woman away from your head!"

My father was laughing now as hard as anyone else, and I was too, and Andy was laughing, and he turned to me and pushed my shoulder and said, "What are you laughing at?" and that made me laugh the harder.

Hally walked off, probably to give someone else a hard time, and my dad pointed toward the spot where he wanted me to set out the brochures. I started putting the brochures in small stacks. The room was filled with loud and cheerful conversations, laughter. I looked up and Mike was there, the necks of two bottles of Coke pinched between the fingers of his broad right hand. He held out a bottle to me, and I took it with a shy nod. He winked and nodded, took a swig from his bottle of Coke, and walked away. I had a swallow, too, and looked over and saw my dad on the other side of the room talking to Richard Healy and Hally and Mitchell. Hally was laughing hard at one of his own jokes, and my father was grinning, his shoulders shaking with barely suppressed laughter, and I could hear Mitchell say, "You ain't right in the head."

I loved these men. How far away from Emma was I at that moment? Certainly I didn't give her a thought. She was a source of joy and wonder for me, but there was a deep feeling of joy here, as well: the joy of home, the joy of being with a group of people who knew me, and, for good and for ill and through thick and thin, were an inextricable part of who I was. I had no such thoughts then, of course. But I was caught by a kind of joy and pride about being part of this group, of being at the meeting and, more to the point, of belonging there.

After a while the meeting got under way. My father talked at length about hunting safety. He emphasized the importance of wearing blaze orange. He talked about planning the hunt carefully beforehand, and sticking to the plan; about knowing where you were heading, and how long you intended to stay out. He stressed the importance of knowing exactly where your hunting partners were at all times, and of not wandering off yourself without letting your partners know. Then my father began telling about an incident from the year before.

One county over, maybe thirty miles away, a man had shot his brother because he mistook him for a turkey. The fellow had walked a little ways off to relieve himself, and the unexpected rustle, the snatch of red clothing that might or might not have looked like a turkey's neck, had caused his brother to fire. The single rifle shot had pierced the man's throat. The shooter ran over, thinking to find a turkey, and found his brother crumpled on the ground, his pants twisted around his knees, dead. Everyone knew the story already. It had enough elements of the macabre, the tragic, to be well known. But my father told it again to good effect.

"Hell of a way to die," I heard Hally say from a few rows behind me. "Get popped while you're taking a crap."

There were a couple of grumbles, some nervous laughter.

"It's not funny, Hally," someone said.

"I know it's not funny," Hally shot back. "It scares the hell out of me."

"Good," my father said brusquely. "It should scare you."

I thought: "Even Emma couldn't have saved him." It was the first time that evening that I had thought of her.

Just then I heard a woman's voice. It seemed that everyone's head turned as mine did.

"Officer," she called to my father as she walked toward the front of the room.

"God help us," I heard someone mutter. Everyone watched her as she walked. She was a young woman, very fair, with light, light blond hair. She was so thin she looked frail. Her jaw was set tight as she walked, her eyes set straight ahead, ignoring the men all around her.

"Go home, Carole Ann," Corey Hughes called out. His voice was flat, not unkind but definite.

"Officer, can I say a few words?" she asked my father. She was standing only a few feet away from me. Her jeans hung loosely on her thin hips. She was wearing an oversize sweater that seemed to engulf her.

For a moment my father didn't speak.

"Aw, for gosh sakes, Singer, we didn't come to listen to her!" This was Lyle Abbott. I knew all these men; I didn't know her. Merwyn Powell was seated next to me, his hands folded lightly on his large belly, a look of quiet disapproval on his face.

"Who is she, Mr. Powell?" I whispered.

"She's a nut. But if I know your father, we're gonna listen to her."

Several of the men were complaining now, but my father already had his hand up. The room settled down.

"Gentlemen, this is a public meeting in a public building. If Miss Proffitt wants to talk to us, briefly," he paused and looked at her. She did not flinch. ". . . then let's give her our full attention."

"Some of you might know . . ." she said softly. Her voice was quavering.

"Speak up, darlin'!" someone from the back called.

"Some of you might know," she said more slowly, loudly, looking down at the floor, then up at the ceiling, and then, suddenly, fixedly, at me. "I'm the president of the local animal rights group."

"Oh for crying out loud!" Chester Lanz started.

My father banged the flat of his hand, once, on the table top, and Chester frowned, and was silent.

"I know you don't want to listen to me. I know you think there's nothing I could say to you that could change how you think about hunting," her voice was shaking. I thought it was nervousness, then realized in an instant that it was anger, a true and deep anger. She took a breath. All at once the anger seemed gone, to be replaced by sadness, resignation. Her voice became too quiet. "You're probably right. There's probably nothing I can say."

"Nothing that we can hear!" Hally shouted, which brought some laughs. Even my father looked down at the floor and smiled.

"Nothing that I can say," she repeated more loudly. "But I want you to listen to Charlie Hatch for a minute."

She gestured toward the back of the room. Charlie was back there, his hands jammed in his pockets.

"Charlie, come on," the woman urged, motioning him toward the front.

Charlie stood quite still. There was a long silence; you could hear the Coke machine buzz.

"How ya doing, Charlie?" Hally called to him. No one laughed.

"Okay, so I was hunting last year, right?" Charlie spoke loudly, apparently to his shoes. "And I was with my friend Landon, ya'll know Landon, and we were up in tree stands, you know, fifteen feet up or something, only we just had the one ladder, and Landon was up in his stand last, about fifty yards away, okay, and so he had the ladder at his stand. And this buck walks underneath me, just, damn, right there," he stopped abruptly. He had been speaking quickly. For the first time he looked up at us. "Right there beneath me, and I shot him."

Charlie stared back at the floor and kept talking. "And I shot him once and I'd have shot him again but my gun jammed. He went down on his forelegs and he was trying to get back up; he was, like, spinning there in place, kneeling on his forelegs, trying to get up, and I hollered for Landon to come over, and, well, he did, he climbed down and come over but it was, I don't know, minutes, four or five or six minutes, and that buck just spun, and struggled, and fell, and tried to get up and couldn't. It took him forever to die, before Landon got there. I just stood up there like I was some god in the sky, some big man that could kill an animal like that. I just watched him. And I knew right then that I shouldn't have ought to shot him, and I tell you, I won't do it again. And that's all that I'm going to say. I mean, if you shoot something . . ." he stopped abruptly. The room was silent. Charlie blinked his eyes, like he was blinking away tears. We waited, and Charlie began again.

"I mean, if you're going to shoot something, well, I just figure . . ." He took a deep breath. "God goes to all this trouble to make a deer, you know? So if you shoot one, just make sure you're prepared to watch it die."

He kicked at the floor, looked up at us, and said, "Good night," in an odd, almost formal tone, and hurried out of the back of the room, shouldering past three people who were lugging in some huge object in a sheet. The sheet was stained with blood. My head swum a moment, and then came crystal clear. Two men and a woman—I didn't know any of them—were lugging a dead deer wrapped in a sheet to the front table. They heaved it with a thud on the table in front of us all. The rank smell from it filled the room.

"She's a pregnant doe," Carole Ann Proffitt said sharply. "One of you shot her two days ago off the back of Mavis Gentry's property. Anybody want to claim it?"

She said this last around my father, who had moved in front of her. The room was in commotion, men moving to see, a chair fell over, someone was cursing.

"Let's go," my father said sharply, to Carole Ann and the people with her. "Outside. Thomas, come with us. Richard," he nodded to Richard Healy, and gestured toward the deer. "Burn that thing."

My father led us down the center of the room. Sherman Kyle, another particular friend of my father's, fell in silently behind us. He was a quiet, lanky man. I was glad to have him there. I don't believe anyone could possibly have come to any harm there; indeed I'm sure Carole Ann and her friends could have left in safety, with no more than some jeering. But as it was, we moved swiftly out of a nearly silent room.

My father took the steps rapidly, the first one down the stairs. I could tell he was angry, a rare state for him. I ended up next to Carole Ann. As we descended the stairs she gripped me by the wrist, hard.

"Don't become like them," she whispered sharply. "You don't have to be like them."

"That's my father," I said, because it was the only thing I could think of to say. He was holding the front door to the firehouse open ahead of us.

We spilled down the steps into the parking lot. The night had grown much colder. After all the activity upstairs, it was strangely quiet outside. It was a muted group that climbed into a couple of pickup trucks and drove out of the firehouse parking lot. My father stood silently watching them go, Sherman Kyle at his side. I didn't realize how angry he was until he spoke.

"Now what the hell did they think they were going to accomplish by that?" he asked sharply, and turned to look to Sherman, and saw me. His face, tight with anger, softened. "Son," he said quietly.

"I don't know," Sherman said, in his slow, easy drawl. "I expect they thought they'd make an impression."

"And what's Charlie Hatch want to get caught up with them for?" my father asked.

Sherman shook his head. "Charlie's a good boy. I can't see that he meant any harm."

"No," my father agreed. He seemed to force a smile. I could see that his anger was fading.

"I'm cold," I said.

Sherman laughed. "I'm a-cold, too," he said, and the three of us went back inside.

Upstairs the evidence of the deer carcass having been there was all but gone. A couple of the men were slowly, methodically cleaning the table up front with wet, soapy sponges. Mitchell was rolling the mop and bucket away, having cleaned a wide path up through the center of the room. The deer itself was gone. Several of the men were still very agitated. Some even questioned if charges couldn't be filed against Carole Ann and her group for disturbing the peace.

"You can swear out a complaint," my father said, his even temper returned. "But I wouldn't bother with it."

They burned the carcass in the little field behind the firehouse. Some of the men went out back to watch, but it wasn't much of a fire, and the night was very cold. I could see the flames from the windows of the meeting room, while my father and I packed up the leftover brochures.

"Need a hand with that box?" It was Sherman Kyle.

"No sir," I said, "thanks, but it's not heavy."

"I hear we'll be going out together next week," Sherman said.

He meant hunting.

"Yes sir," I said quietly, moving the brochures around in the box, not looking up.

"Well that's good," Sherman said. "That's real good."

Chapter 6

In the days that followed, I was alternately certain that I would not go hunting with Sherman Kyle, my father, and their friends, and then so unsure of what I would do that I felt ill with doubt and anxiety. I missed Emma. I walked out into the woods one day after school, but Emma was not there to meet me. The woods themselves felt strange, or I was a stranger to them. I was so preoccupied with my one great dilemma that I was not seeing the landscape around me, feeling the air, sensing the ground beneath my feet. The quiet, the sense of harmony and order that was so basic to my time walking in the woods, especially with Emma, was lost to me now. It could scarcely be literally true, but it seemed to me that there were more brambles, more impenetrable thickets, steeper and rockier hills, than there had been just the week before.

The morning of my birthday came. I had never spoken to my father again about whether I would go hunting with him. He talked a lot that week about where to go hunting, what to bring, what the weather might be like, what sort of luck there would be. There seemed to be an unspoken assumption that of course I would be going too.

So, at five in the morning my father came in my room with two bulky parcels.

"Happy birthday, son," he said.

I hadn't been asleep. I knew what was in the parcels. I knew what was about to happen. I felt powerless. No, that's not right. I wanted to feel powerless. I didn't want to be responsible for whatever happened.

The shotgun was beautiful, like the one I had shot, but even lovelier. It was the perfect size for me, shorter than a normal shotgun, and lighter. Its weight and balance were perfect. The stock was hand-turned, the wood a rich, glowing red, like silk to the touch. I couldn't wait to shoot it. I didn't want to shoot it. I didn't know what I wanted. The other parcel contained my bright orange hunting jacket. It fit perfectly, like I had known it would.

"Breakfast is on," my father said. He gave my leg a little slap, and left the room.

This is the time, I thought. This is the time when you have to make up your mind. I wished idly that there was a door that led from my room to the backyard. Then I could have simply plunged into the woods and spent the day there, hiding. It was a pointless wish.

I felt flat and defeated. I got out of bed and quite mechanically washed and dressed myself. When I was done I stood in front of my bed and looked at the shotgun lying there, the hunting jacket beside it.

"Well," I said out loud, to Emma or to myself I do not know. "Anyway, I'm sorry."

I hefted the gun into the crook of my arm, picked up the jacket, and walked out into the kitchen.

My mother gave me a strange, concerned look, but didn't say anything. My father was cheerful, unusually noisy for him. I half expected him to break into song. My mother was quiet, and I was resolute, grim.

Finally, she placed her hand on my wrist, lightly, and said "You be careful today, okay?"

"He'll be fine," my father said. "He's just nervous."

"Of course he's nervous," my mother said.

"I'm okay," I said, which may have been my first and only words at the breakfast table.

We were meeting a few men at the firehouse. I stared out the window as we drove along. It was very dark out, but there were lights on in a lot of the houses.

"Lots of people going to call in sick to work today," my father said with a chuckle. "First day of hunting season—they ought to go on and make it a holiday, have done with it."

I didn't answer. I was wondering where Emma was. In a way, I was wondering if she really existed. I hadn't seen her in so long. It all seemed like a dream: Emma and Reggie, Abigail and her hip, all the events of the past few weeks. It all seemed so long ago, so strange and so terribly unlikely. I felt miserable.

The men at the firehouse didn't help. They made a big fuss over this being my first time hunting, and would I have live shells in my gun, and did I know the difference between a deer and a stump? They had a big play argument over what I would shoot first, my foot, or one of them. They made me angry, and embarrassed. I was angry, too, at my father. He had told me that the men knew I was coming that day, but they acted like they had never heard about it.

My pride was hurt. But it was more than that. After weeks of turmoil over whether I would go hunting, my nerves were frayed past the breaking point. Now that I was there with the men, I desperately wanted to be accepted; I couldn't see that their teasing was in a way a part of that acceptance. I couldn't see past my need to be with them, regardless of the cost. I didn't even admire all the men there. My father and Mr. Kyle, yes. But they weren't the ones having the most fun at my expense.

Harmon Williams was a big, loud man who was also a county deputy. I could tell he envied my father, envied his easygoing nature and his popularity. He loved to tease my father, to catch him out in some mistake (which was rare enough), to tell stories on him in ways that they didn't really happen. My father laughed along. He seemed to think Harmon was okay. Harmon was dressed all in camouflage, with black grease paint under his eyes. My father didn't like that; he thought the camouflage could make it difficult for us to see him.

"That's the point," Harmon said with a laugh. "If you can see me, for damn sure the deer can too."

"Someday you're going to get a butt full of shot," my father muttered. He and I were both wearing our huge, bright orange coats.

Harmon brought a 30:06 rifle with a fancy sighting scope, which my father also didn't like. A rifle's range was too great, my father said; if you missed your target heaven knows how far the bullet would travel, or what it might hit. But Harmon would hunt with nothing else. He didn't want to lose a trophy buck because it was too far away for a shotgun to reach.

Then there was Andy Powell, who carried an old shotgun because it was all he had. Andy was the type of person who never really got the hang of anything. He thought Harmon was a scream. Anything Harmon said, Andy would repeat, at least twice, and laugh like mad. Harmon got more fun out of teasing me than he had probably had in years, and Andy laughed and laughed. Sherman just smiled, now and then, and my father smiled and patted me on the back and shoved my hat around on my head.

Sherman Kyle was tall, thin, and quiet. Next to my father I'm sure he was the best hunter. My father insisted Sherman was the better woodsman, and Sherman just said, "Naw, naw, that's you." Sherman wore a red plaid shirt and a red plaid jacket and, in deference to my father perhaps, a blaze orange cap. He carried a shotgun, "in case we see some turkey out there," he said. A rifle's bullet will destroy a turkey, leaving nothing worth cleaning to eat, where shotgun pellets will not. In truth, I don't think he cared for rifles either, for the same reason as my father, though he wasn't inclined to say so.

The last to arrive was Merwin Powell, Andy's brother, who rolled into the firehouse parking lot about a half an hour late. No one expected him to be on time. Merwin was a big, jowly, slow man who was always late for everything. I had always liked Merwin. His great size and quiet manner somehow felt comfortable and safe for me. But even he started in on me.

"We bringin' the boy?" Merwin asked.

My stomach twisted into a tighter knot; we'd have to go through it all again.

"Yeah, li'l peckerwood here," Harmon said. "Maybe he can catch him a squirrel."

"Li'l peckerwood," Andy said, and guffawed.

"I don't much care to hunt with a young 'un," Merwin said. "Not in a group."

"He'll be fine," my father said. "I've taught him."

"Yeah, er, tha's fine, but I don't much . . ."

"Probably just shoot a stump!" Andy said.

" . . . care for huntin' with young 'uns," Merwin continued.

"A stump, or us!" Andy said.

I was battling back tears. If I cried I would never hear the end of it.

"So where we fixing to go?" Sherman asked. "It's about time we started."

"I was thinking east, off Highway 6," my father said.

"There's some good land there, and it's open to hunters."

"Aw, everyone's going to be up there, Singer," Harmon complained. "That's no good at all."

"Too many up there today," said Andy. "Scare off all the deer."

"We could go on back to my place," Merwin said. He had a couple of hundred acres just north of town.

"What 'a you think, peckerwood," Harmon said to me, and winked at Andy. "You want 'a shoot some 'a Merwin's stumps?"

"I know where there's the biggest buck you ever saw," I flashed back at him, angry, unthinking, aware only of Andy's raucous laughter. "Up south of Harrow Point. I know where there's a mess 'a deer up there."

"It's good hunting up there," Sherman said.

"Won't be many folks driving up that far," my father said. "You might have hit on the place, Tom."

I was breathing fast. The men were quiet a moment, and I waited for the terror of what I had done to grip me. I felt hollow, though, and suddenly weak.

"No, I don't know," I mumbled. "There's probably nothing up there."

"Naw, the boy's got a good idea, I guess," said Merwin. "Yeah, I know a way in up there, just a few miles south of Harrow Point. Nice and open. Yeah, son, you got a good idea."

It was decided. I felt powerless to stop what I had started. We piled into Harmon's beat up old Land Rover and headed up Highway 12 to Harrow Point. My heart was pounding against my ribs. But the men were happy. They actually complimented me, each of them in his way, on choosing Harrow Point, once we were headed that way. It only took us twenty minutes or so and we were parked, and then unloaded, and then had plunged into the woods.

On any other day the woods would have felt perfect to me. The air was cold but not bitter, the sky overcast, everything still and quiet. We made such a lot of racket, though, the six of us. Merwin and Andy especially seemed to crash along through the underbrush, snapping twigs and crunching leaves. It made me glad. Surely the deer would hear us and run far, far away, to safety.

I was starting to recognize familiar terrain, where Emma and I had walked less than two weeks before. That day seemed years ago. Suddenly we came upon the meadow, Reggie's meadow, and I thought my heart would stop from fear. But the meadow was empty, just the tall grasses and low shrubs, motionless in the still air.

Something in the stillness of the air, the utter quiet of that moment, brought me up short. It was as if there had been a voice in my head talking non-stop for the past few weeks that had suddenly, abruptly fallen silent. Sherman Kyle had been walking beside me; now he pulled a few paces ahead, his footfalls sounding like small explosions. In the midst of that great silence, without thinking, I knelt down and put my palm, gently, upon the earth. It was alive.

"Danger." I heard this word, soft as a whisper, fluttering inside my chest.

My head snapped up. I stood, and looked back across the meadow from where we had come.

"Man-child?"

It was Reggie, thirty yards or so behind us. The entire universe stood still. I mouthed the word "run."

"Go on, son," Sherman whispered. He was beside me. "You seen him. You go on."

No, I thought. No.

"No," I said aloud. And then I yelled: "No! Run, run!" and I ran toward Reggie, waving my arms in the air like some big, crazy bird. I seemed to be running in slow motion. I could see my father, far to my right, his face turned to me, and closer to me, not twenty feet away, Harmon, startled, almost stumbling, but at the same time raising his rifle to his shoulder. I ran harder, trying to shout, but I only covered a few more feet of ground when all at once there was a pop, and a raging, buzzing sound, and I was flying, burning, tumbling, and crashed through the brush, face down in the dirt.

"Oh Jesus, oh Jesus!" I heard.

"I didn't . . . oh Jesus!" It was Harmon's voice, in a pitch much higher than normal. "I didn't see him!" Harmon was almost shrieking, from some far distance away. Harmon shot me, I thought. Harmon shot me. It took a while for the thought to sink in.

"Thomas!" I heard. It was my father. I wanted to answer him.

I felt so odd. I felt a great burning in my back, only

it was as if it were someone else's back. I was like a balloon deflating. I realized I was cold. I was lying very still and yet I felt like I was running in place, or, no, just that my heart, my body was rushing toward something. I had a mouthful of dirt and leaves, and I couldn't spit it out. The wind was rushing and I was cold. I couldn't taste the dirt.

"Thomas!"

I was looking up at my father. Then there was a great commotion, they were trying to lift me, and half dropped me, and there were sounds, yelling, and they set me down.

"Oh Thomas, why?" I heard. "Why are you here?"

Emma. She was leaning over me, pressing my shoulders to the ground with her hands, looking me at me with great concentration. She looked up and around, shaking her head, her face creased with dismay, the light flying off her hair. I felt I was a tiny spot, miles away from her. I wanted to walk to her, but it was so far; it would take forever. There were some things I needed to tell her. Finally she pulled me up into her arms, holding me, rocking me.

"It's all right," she said. "My dear Thomas, it's all right."

She held me and I was almost broken by the pain that burned through me. I grabbed her as tightly as I could. It wasn't just my pain, but hers as well—ours. We seemed in a world apart for just that fraction of time. But then there was another commotion around me, around us; the men were trying to separate us.

I tried to cry out. I felt my head flop backward. I could see my father, poised above us. His hands were on my shoulders, grasping me, ready to pull me from Emma.

"Let me hold him!" I heard her cry. Her voice was raspy, strange.

"We should get him to the truck," I heard Sherman say. "Now."

They tried to pull Emma to her feet. She was still holding me. I was clutching her with what strength I had. I tried to say the word "No." I tried to hold on to her. Emma fell to one knee, cradling me even tighter against her.

"Give me time," she whispered. "A little time."

My father was trying to pull Emma and me apart, but for the briefest moment he hesitated. The moment became an eternity. For the first time in my life I saw real fear in my father's eyes. I was willing him to make the right decision. I couldn't speak or move but my heart called to him: Let her hold me. I could see anguish on his face. He was staring into my eyes. How could I make him understand? Finally, his eyes left mine and he looked past me into the trees beyond.

"God help me," he said quietly.

Then, more loudly: "Let her be. Merwin, give Sherman the keys. Run, bring the vehicle through as close as you can."

"Can you walk with him?" my father asked Emma.

"Not now," she breathed. "Soon."

"Run, Sherman," my father said sharply.

I collapsed with relief ever further into Emma's embrace, and closed my eyes. Then all was darkness, and silence.

Chapter 7

At first, I was simply aware of being aware. No sound or sight or feeling. It seemed to me that a long time ago something important had happened, but I couldn't remember what it might have been. Gradually, I noticed that I was warm. I realized that there was a very small circle of light some distance away from me. For a time, that was all I was aware of; I was warm, instead of cold, and there was this small circle of light.

It's like being at the bottom of a well, looking up, I thought.

I sensed, almost like one picks out a faint aroma on the breeze, that there was a great deal of activity somewhere far away from me. I wasn't aware of pain, or of having a body at all. But then I remembered: Harmon shot me.

"Emma, where am I?" I asked, or thought, or thought aloud.

I wasn't really expecting an answer, but I got one.

"Emma's done all she can for you," came a deep, old, voice that I had heard only once, but was sure I recognized. It wasn't so much that I heard it now. I felt it, felt the voice within me.

"Mr. Nash?"

"Thomas."

There was a long silence.

"Where are we?"

"That depends on you, young man."

He was angry with me. There was no tenderness in his voice, none of the affection I heard so often in Emma's voice.

"I'm sorry. I'm really sorry."

"That's as may be. What are you going to do now?"

Another silence.

"Harmon shot me."

"That he did. What do you think about that?"

"He didn't mean to. He should have been more careful. I should have been more careful."

"Hmmm."

"I shouldn't have been there at all."

"Emma is of the opinion that you needed to be there."

"Is she all right?"

"It depends. Everything changes. You might bear that in mind, young man. Everything changes."

"Yes sir. I am sorry."

All this time there was just this warm darkness, and this small circle of light. It wasn't so much that we were speaking. I couldn't see Mr. Nash; I couldn't see any part of myself for that matter, or hear the sound of my voice. In a strange, unsettling way it was how I might have imagined talking to God would be, although I had never thought of God as being so cross, or having such a deep country accent.

"Mr. Nash, am I dead?"

"Dead," he repeated, as if considering the word. "No son, you're not dead. Let me ask you again, what are you going to do now?"

"I . . . I don't know that I can do anything. I want to see Emma, to see if she's all right. I want to tell Harmon that I'm okay. I want to see my dad. I don't know. I want to see you."

I felt a bolt of pain shoot through me, more fierce than anything I had ever felt in my life, and that tiny sphere of light exploded in a silent fireball that completely engulfed me in an instant. I lurched forward, and then fell back, and realized for the first time that I was lying on a bed, or a stretcher. The white sphere of light was gone. Everything was a faint, faint white, a dark white, if such a thing is possible. I was lying back, the pain ebbing, ebbing, unable to move. And there was Mr. Nash.

"I know it hurts, son," he said, a gentleness appearing in his voice for the first time. "It's going to hurt for a while."

He laid his hand on my arm. He was old, in his nineties I would have guessed, but his hand was strong.

His face was long and deeply wrinkled; he was nearly bald; he had very big ears. I liked the look of him. The pain bucked through me again, and faded more quickly. We were alone in what seemed to be a little alcove, a strange, dark-white space suspended all by itself somewhere.

Mr. Nash stood beside me, and gently pressed his hand on my stomach and up across my chest.

"I don't like the feel of your back," he said. "You'll need to work with that."

"Yes, sir," I answered, my eyes closed against the pain, my breath coming in sharp little pieces. I could feel his hands working through me; everywhere he worked there was so much pain.

"You can stand a little pain; that's good," Mr. Nash said, to himself as much as to me it seemed, then more loudly. "The bullet about destroyed one of your vertebra. Emma reshaped it and I've done what I can but there's some damage there. You're going to carry that pain with you."

"It's all right," I said.

"It'll have to be," he said.

His hands worked slowly, deftly. I felt like a lump of dough, a loaf of bread he was gently kneading into just the perfect shape. I watched him, mesmerized, knowing he was doing just what Emma had taught me about. My breathing came easier and fuller.

"How are you doing, there, son?" Mr. Nash asked.

"I'm fine, I'm fine," I said quickly, not wanting him to stop.

"Yes, well, fine as you'll get right now," he said, and stepped back from me.

"We've about got you ready to go back to your family," he said.

"Thank you sir," I answered, hesitant.

"What is it, then?"

"I want to keep learning the things Emma taught me," I said. "I want . . ." I came up short; Mr. Nash was eyeing me with such critical appraisal.

"I want to do what you do," I said weakly.

"It's best to forget all that," he said.

"Forget?"

"You're young," he said. "You have things to do. Go to school, meet girls, find some work for yourself. Maybe someday, down the road, we'll talk again."

"I know the work I want to do," I said, and with the greatest of effort I held his gaze, my eyes locked on his. Everything Emma had taught me, everything that I wanted someday to be, welled up inside me and forced me to withstand the fierce, relentless power of Mr. Nash's gaze. To the surprise of us both, perhaps, my determination held. Finally, finally, he smiled, looked down at my chest, and began tapping there—hard, slowly, with his sharp forefinger.

"I'll leave that up to Emma, then," he said. Tap. Tap. Tap. "Work from your heart, Thomas, if you're going to work. Always from your heart." Tap. Tap. Tap. "Empty yourself of opinions. Empty yourself of pride." Tap. Tap. Tap. "And, Thomas, the next time someone asks you—"

"Yes sir?"

"Say 'I . . . '"

TAP

"'Bring . . . '"

TAP

"'Strength!'"

And with that he slapped the living hell out of me.

I shot bolt upright in bed and slammed my forehead into the forehead of the unfortunate young emergency room doctor who was leaning over me, listening to my chest through a stethoscope. I fell back on the bed and grabbed my head, the great wooden "thonk!" of our collision still echoing in both our ears, I'm sure. The pain was such that it made me laugh. I looked up and saw so many concerned, surprised, anxious faces that I almost laughed again. And just behind the cluster of doctors and nurses and technicians I saw a balding old man in an old weathered coat, his finger to the side of his nose—our little secret, the gesture said—wink at me and leave the trauma room.

"Wow," I said to the doctor, rubbing my forehead, smiling. "Sorry about that."

He smiled back at me, a look of frank astonishment in his eyes. "I'm okay," he said. "How do you feel?"

"I'm fine," I said, looking at all the faces peering at me. I tried to move a little in the small stretcher. Mr. Nash wasn't kidding about my back.

"My back hurts," I said.

"Heh," the doctor suppressed a laugh, which was more than some of the others did. They seemed a pretty happy bunch, the nurses and all. There were so many people in such a small space, all staring at me. I found myself suddenly wanting to be left alone.

"You're a very lucky fellow," the doctor told me. "We thought for a minute there . . . well, it doesn't matter what we thought. You're a very lucky fellow," he said again.

"I want to see Emma," I said.

"Emma?" the doctor looked around. "Is that the woman who . . . "

At that moment my father burst through the door and plowed through the people around me, my mother close in his wake. He took me in his arms, holding me. I kept telling him that I was okay, but he wouldn't let go. He was crying, my mother was crying. It scared me almost, and, I'm sad to say, I was embarrassed that they were crying over me in front of all those strangers.

It seems awful, or hard-hearted, to recall now, but I felt a bit exasperated by the whole thing. I assured everyone that I was all right, and somehow I expected that to be enough, that we could just leave the hospital and go home. But of course to the doctors and nurses I had more or less miraculously come back from the brink of death. I soon learned that a thirty-caliber bullet had passed through me, clean through, with a big entry wound and a great gaping exit wound in my chest. By all accounts, I should have died on the spot. But they assumed that clearly the bullet had missed hitting any major organs; and, by some process that no one could understand, no one but me, I had only two raw, red, fleshy scars, front and back, rather than the two open wounds logic required I should have. It was like there was a certain audacity to what I had done, surviving in this way; the people at the hospital were delighted with me and baffled by me at the same time. And they simply would not leave me alone.

I wanted to see Emma.

I told them, leaving out rather a lot, who Emma was, and the staff said they would set about trying to reach her family. At first I couldn't get them to tell me what was happening with her, but finally they admitted that she was not doing well. She was upstairs, on the floor above me, in the Intensive Care Unit. I badgered the nurses relentlessly to let me go see her. My father spoke with the doctor. They came together to my bedside.

"I guess I can't think of a reason why you shouldn't visit your friend," the doctor said, frowning slightly with evident concern.

"I'll be fine," I said bluntly.

"It's okay, Tom," my father said. He went and got a wheelchair, and helped me into it. He wheeled me to an elevator, and we went up to the next floor in silence.

When we got to the door of her room I craned my neck around, wincing from the pain in my back, to look up at my father.

"I need to see her alone," I said.

"Okay," he said quietly. He didn't release his grip on the wheelchair.

"Tell her . . ." he began, but then he shook his head. After a moment he gave me a faint smile, and touched my face with his hand. Then he walked slowly down the hall to the elevator.

I opened the door to her room and slowly, awkwardly wheeled myself in. She was so old. That was the first thing I saw. She seemed to have aged twenty years that afternoon. Her face was pale and oddly puffy. I fought back tears. The door slipped shut behind me, and for a long while I just sat there and looked at her. I was too sad, too ashamed to take her hand, or to speak. I sat hunched in the wheelchair, wishing to heaven that the whole thing had not happened, that I had never gone hunting that day, that Emma was well and strong.

"Thomas?"

Her voice was faint; it startled me to attention. Her face was toward me, a slight smile on her lips.

"Emma? Are you okay?"

"I've been better," she said slowly.

I think my face, already downcast, fell even further.

"I'm fine, child," she said. "I'll always be fine. Don't worry."

"I'm so sorry. I'm so sorry for what happened."

I was crying. She lifted her hand, and let it fall. I put my hand on top of hers.

"Everything will be well," she said. "Leave me for a while, but don't worry. Think healing thoughts."

I managed to wheel myself out of the room, banging into a side table, the wall, tears flowing down my face.

Downstairs, there was concern and repeated questions over my crying. Everyone seemed intensely aware of everything I did or said, of every expression on my face, as if I might suddenly decide to die after all. They were moving me to a room on the same floor as Emma, to keep me for a day or two of "observation." I found it intolerable that they wouldn't simply leave me alone.

It took some time to get me into my room. My parents stayed quite a while, not talking much, but clearly not wanting to leave. I wanted to be alone. I told them I was tired, and they left, reluctantly, so that I could sleep. Once they were gone I began, with almost feverish intensity, to try and generate a circle of healing that would encompass and support Emma, cursing myself all the while for not practicing the week before as she had so particularly asked me to do. But I was exhausted, and in spite of my intention to maintain this vigil through the night, I quickly fell into a deep, deep sleep.

I opened my eyes, suddenly and completely awake, sometime far into the middle of the night. I knew, without a sense of anxiety, that Emma needed to see me, right then. The hospital was quiet. I could hear a distant "beep—beep—beep," a muffled cough. Without a thought as to explaining myself to any doctor or nurse I might see, I stole out of bed and walked directly, silently down the hall, to the adjacent wing and Emma's room. No one saw me. Emma was awake, waiting for me.

"Hello, my dear," she said.

"How are you feeling?" I asked. She looked a little

better, I guess, but if anything she looked older still, and she was eerily pale.

"I think I'm going to move on," she said simply, and even though I knew what she meant, it took a moment for the words to register.

"Emma, no," I said.

"It's not the end; don't worry. Do you remember, Thomas, I told you once that all the animals I help go on to die someday?"

"I remember."

"Well, it's the same with me, and with you. We have to die. But the work we do goes on. We go on . . . with the work. Once you start, you never finish. I'm sure of that."

"Will I be able to see you?"

"No, dear. Not any time soon."

"But I saw Mr. Nash," I protested. "I talked to him."

"I know. He told me. But he's much further along the path than I am. I don't know what to tell you. There are so many things I don't understand."

I shook my head, "No."

"Don't worry, dear," she said, and then she added, "although I admit, I'm a little afraid."

"Afraid?" I asked, alarmed. She always seemed so calm and confident. "Afraid of what?"

"Dying," she said simply. "Mr. Nash says not to be, and really he should know, but I can't help it. He says that life, and death, is a little different for everyone: no two creatures are just the same, he says. So I don't know how it will be for me. I asked Mr. Nash and he said 'How should I know? Everything changes.'"

"He said that to me, too," I said.

"He says that a lot. I guess I'm about to understand a little better what he means."

"Emma, I can't stand it if you go. I feel like it's all my fault."

She patted the side of her bed. "Sit here," she said. I settled gently on the edge of the bed, not wanting to jostle her. She took my hand in hers.

"I know I'm going to forget half the things I wanted to tell you," she said.

She started talking very quietly, sometimes with her eyes closed, sometimes looking up at the ceiling, sometimes looking directly, piercingly, at me. She was very still, her breathing shallow. I leaned close to her, not wanting to miss anything. She talked a while about her childhood, about growing up outside of Harrow Point, about the family store. She told me again about her husband, her children.

"I had a normal life, I guess. A full, normal life. It was hard back then, harder in some ways than now because you had to work such long hours, always, just to get by. But, Thomas, it was a normal life I had, and I'm afraid that you'll lose that, by my teaching you things so early."

"It's okay," I said.

"It's not though. Forgive me, dear, but you don't know enough yet to say so. Balance is so important."

"Balance?" I thought she meant something like "not tipping over."

"A balanced life. There's so much suffering in the

world, Thomas. We can only touch the surface of it, emptying the ocean a thimble at a time. It's all we can do, but it's what we do. That's what I've been teaching you to do—giving you, well," she smiled, "a better thimble. But there is so much joy, too, and beauty, and simple, commonplace, everyday wonder and delight that should be yours too. And the sorrows, the little human idiocies—Thomas, you have to understand, what happened today . . . "

"I'm so sorry," I said, suddenly in tears. "I never should have been there."

"Yes, you should have," she said forcefully. "I was the one who shouldn't have been there. Or . . . I pushed you into a place you weren't ready to be. You were out with your father, with your friends, trying to learn whether you were a hunter or not. But I had thrown everything out of balance for you."

"But if I hadn't . . . "

She cut me off. "You saved Reggie. You intercepted that bullet. You did. I'm proud of you for that. And you learned, for yourself, that you're not a hunter. You had to learn for yourself."

I cried then. I still felt guilty, but what she said helped. She talked on. She told me more about the techniques of healing. It's surprisingly simple, really: a natural human gift. She talked at greater length about the state of mind, the state of heart, for the healing to be healthy and effective. She kept coming back to humility, and gentleness, and the willingness to put my feelings and opinions to one side for the sake of whoever it was that was in front of me. She was repeating herself, at the end, so anxious was she that I should understand. Finally she relaxed, and we were quiet for a while.

"Here then," she said, after a time. "Lean closer."

When I did, she grasped the back of my neck, tightly, and pulled me towards her. Her grip was so tight it hurt. There are times, in truth, when the place she gripped me hurts me still. She held me there, so tightly, and then she pulled me even closer, until our foreheads touched. Her candle to mine, I think now. Her candle to mine. She told me one last thing, which I will not share, and then she said she loved me.

"I love you, too."

"Thomas, I'm scared," she said. She was trembling.

"Emma!"

Then her grip on my neck, so iron tight, loosened, and her breathing eased to almost nothing. She relaxed. Everything about her relaxed, like a great sinking, a fading.

"He's here," she whispered. With a faint chuckle, she died.

They let me go home the next day. There wasn't any reason to keep me; my wounds were two big fresh pink scars, front and back. The wounds were healed, but my chest ached from sorrow. Nothing in the world could help my sadness at losing Emma.

It seemed so clear to me that we had been building toward something, Emma and I. She was leading me to a place that I couldn't now get to, on my own. I kept going through everything she had told me in the weeks that I knew her, trying to remember every word. She had been the embodiment of wisdom and magic to me, and for the brief time we were together it had seemed that a little of her magic had rubbed off on me. Now I was just an ordinary boy in a little country town, lucky to be alive.

There was such a lot of fuss and trouble over the shooting. I was this marvel at school: it seemed like half the kids were afraid to talk to me, and the other half wouldn't stop asking me questions about what had happened. My father, for his part, was adamant about pressing charges against Harmon for the reckless discharge of a firearm. Of course, the shooting had just been a foolish accident; I felt that it was at least as much my fault as Harmon's for running in front of him that way. But my father would not budge, which was a misery for me at the time. The whole community was in an uproar over the notion that a hunting accident could lead to legal charges. Some people thought it made perfect sense, and some thought the idea was practically sacrilegious. A state senator actually called the house one evening to try and talk my father out of pressing charges. I begged him to let the matter drop. Finally, to appease me, and being glad, I know, to have his son home and safe, my father relented.

All the attention and controversy was difficult for me. The only hint of peace I could find came from walking in the woods; but it was there that I most deeply missed Emma. After school I headed out through the fields at the edge of town, straight to the base of that same little bramble-covered hill where I first met her. I combed the woods, searching for some trace that she had ever been there. I have no idea what I thought I might find. Each night I came home sad, tired, with an aching back that I knew would never quite heal—came home to parents who couldn't help but beam at their son, restored to them from the dead.

On the first Saturday after the shooting I left the house early and just started walking. I wasn't conscious of where I wanted to go until I had been in the woods nearly an hour. I didn't go up as far as Reggie's meadow, but veered, instead, over toward Harrow Point, and Emma's motor court.

When I got there, the place seemed deserted. I walked past the row of cabins, to the last one, where Emma had lived. I pressed my face to the window to look inside. It was nearly empty, just a broom leaning against the living room wall and a couple of cardboard boxes stacked unevenly in the middle of the floor.

"They already been and took her things," a thin, reedy voice said.

I turned quickly, startled, to find a thin old woman in a stained, old winter parka, her arms crossed against her chest, an unlit cigarette in the fingers of one hand. Abigail was walking up behind her, a little ways off still, moving slowly, limping.

"Her family took her stuff," the woman said again.

"What's in the boxes?" I asked.

"Kitchen things, cleaning things. Her family took her stuff."

"Okay," I said. "Hey, Abigail." The old dog had finally reached us. I bent down and patted her. I pulled my hand back sharply. Abigail slumped against my leg.

"Leave the boy alone, Abby," the woman said. "Stupid old dog."

"No, she's okay," I said. Gently, so gently, I reached down and stroked her again.

"Well, her family took her stuff," the old woman said a final time, and shuffled away.

I knelt down beside Abigail, nervous.

"You're a bit overdue for a treatment, aren't you, old girl?" I said, trying to sound confident, but it was all I could do to breathe. In that first touch I had felt the searing pain in her hip that she endured so patiently. The image of that pain was vivid to me, and the image of the tiny distance we might take it, where it wouldn't hurt so much. I could feel my hands warming, warming. Of course, nothing like this had happened to me since Emma died, but I remembered, or knew somehow instinctively, what I should do.

"It's okay, Abby," I said, my hands moving over her back, her hips. At once she leaned heavily against me.

It didn't take me long to ease the pain in her hip. She had a lot of experience with this sort of healing, after all, and I had worked with her that one time before. It was a good, odd feeling to push her away from me, gently, and pat her rump. I looked around. The first time I had helped Abigail I was completely exhausted when I finished, but now I felt ready for more. Of course, there was no more.

I walked home, feeling flat, strange. Was this what my friendship with Emma was for? So I could take care of an old arthritic dog? Humility, Emma taught me. Put your opinions and wishes to one side. Well, if this was all I was meant to do, help Abigail with her hip, then so be it.

Of course that was not all. I had learned, learned in my heart's core, that I could never be a hunter. My father understood without my having to tell him. When I came home from the hospital, my new shotgun was gone. He told me that he had decided to give up hunting as well. I told him there was no need for him to quit hunting, but he could not be moved on this one. The sight of me lying in the dirt, he said, had cured him for all time of the desire to hunt. The truth is, his decision made me glad.

The next couple of Saturdays I walked up to Harrow Point to tend to Abigail. Finally, I asked the old woman I had talked to there, the manager of the little set of cottages, if I could have Abigail. She certainly didn't mind, and my parents came around easily enough. We lived out in the country, after all. One dog more or less didn't make much difference.

Abigail and Toby got along well, and as Abby settled into the house, her hip seemed to improve a bit, and her coat got thicker and shinier. She was a happy old dog. I still walked in the woods almost every afternoon, and most weekends, but nothing in particular happened out there. Sometimes Abigail would come with me, and we would make our way along very slowly, in deference to her age, and I would think of Emma, and try once again to think through the things that she taught me.

When spring came, it was time for baseball season. I was supposed to move up from Little League to Junior League that year, which was a big deal in our town. I have to say, the summer before I had positively lived for baseball. But playing baseball would mean giving up some of my time walking in the woods, which I was reluctant to do. I kept thinking that I would come upon an injured animal one day and be able to help it the way I could help Abigail.

I thought hard about the things Emma and Mr. Nash told me about balance, about having a normal life. I spent hours debating with myself over whether I should play Junior League baseball or not. I decided that Emma would want me to play, so I signed up.

The first day of practice was a gorgeous spring day, the sun shining brightly, the air deliciously warm, the outfield grass a rich, deep green. I loved the sounds and smells of baseball. Near the end of the practice, the coach let us play a short scrimmage game, which was what all the kids most wanted to do. I was playing right field, focusing completely on the action before me, as happy as I had been in many months.

The field was part of a park at the south edge of town. The road comes out in a big, wide turn at the bottom of the hill, to where the park sits down by the river. Cars would go by now and then, but I was wrapped up in the play and never gave the traffic any particular notice. But then, from the corner of my eye, I saw a little hound dog trotting intently along the side of the road. I smiled and turned back toward the infield, when the hair moved on the back of my neck. I dropped my glove, turned, and started loping out toward the roadway.

I was too late. Everything was happening at once. I turned and began running as a car came down the hill and around the turn much too fast, hitting the shoulder of the road, throwing gravel in its wake as the driver tried to pull the car back onto the road. The little dog never broke stride. The sound of the impact was sickening. The dog was thrown twenty feet or more.

I knelt by the small broken body, trying to catch my breath, feeling an almost frantic sense of fear and pain. It took me a moment to realize that I was intercepting the terror of the dog, who clearly couldn't know what had happened to him.

"It's okay," I said, and tried to think. My hands were shaking. I felt sick to my stomach. I was so afraid.

"It's all right, Thomas," Emma said. "Now, see if you have anything to work with."

"Emma!" I spun around, looking. I had heard her voice as plain as day, but there was no one else nearby, just some of the boys running out toward me from the baseball diamond.

"Yes dear, I'm with you," Emma said, her voice warm and clear from somewhere inside my chest. "But let's mind the dog."

I nodded, trying to focus, trying not to cry. I ran my hands over the dog's coat. He shuddered, his wet brown eyes open, blood seeping onto the gravel underneath him.

"I think it's okay," I said. "I think I can do it."

The dog's spirit was pure fear and pain, almost overwhelming me in its intensity. I tried to soothe him, stroking him lightly, saying "shhh," sensing more clearly the internal damage and how things could be set right.

"Gently, Thomas."

"Yes, thank you. I remember."

Some of the other boys had come up behind me by then. "That's so gross," I heard one of them say. The coach arrived next.

"Singer, the dog's dead. Leave it be."

"No, he's just stunned," I said. I was hunched over the little body, trying to shield him.

"Easy, boy," I said quietly. "Easy, now." I could feel his spirit waver a moment, frightened, but not resisting me so much. I leaned closer, cradling the small dog against my chest, steadying myself, emptying myself.

"I bring strength," I whispered, and set carefully, gently to work.

About the Author

Peter Walpole is a poet, book reviewer, and National Public Radio (NPR) essayist. *The Healer of Harrow Point* is his first book. He lives with his wife in Virginia.

Hampton Roads Publishing Company

. . . for the evolving human spirit

Hampton Roads Publishing Company
publishes books on a variety of subjects including
metaphysics, health, complementary medicine,
visionary fiction, and other related topics.

For a copy of our latest catalog,
call toll-free, 800-766-8009,
or send your name and address to:

Hampton Roads Publishing Company, Inc.
1125 Stoney Ridge Road
Charlottesville, VA 22902
e-mail: hrpc@hrpub.com
www.hrpub.com